SALT ON HER TONGUE

ADVANCE PRAISE FOR *SALT ON HER TONGUE*

"In an insular Maritime village, where secrets run as deep as the sea, Detective Kes Morris is drawn into a series of crimes weaving together small-town tensions, political intrigue, and an international reach. *Salt on Her Tongue* is a riveting blend of suspense, atmosphere and raw emotion. At its heart is Morris—fierce, flawed, and relentless—as unforgettable as the mystery she's determined to unravel. C. S. Porter's sharp prose and tight plot pull you in from the first page and refuse to let go. Haunting, gripping, and impossible to put down, *Salt on Her Tongue* is a must-read for fans of literary crime fiction."
TOM RYAN, AUTHOR OF EDGAR AWARD NOMINEE *THE TREASURE HUNTERS CLUB*

PRAISE FOR *BENEATH HER SKIN*
WINNER, HOWARD ENGEL AWARD FOR BEST CRIME NOVEL SET IN CANADA

"A truly compelling mystery about a series of grisly murders in a lovely east coast town. The writing is superb, the novel tightly plotted...Porter has created an authentic, fully-realized character in Detective Morris, and we'll want to hear from her again." **ANNE EMERY, ARTHUR ELLIS AWARD–WINNING AUTHOR OF *THOUGH THE HEAVENS FALL***

"My goodness, this is an extraordinary work.... A stunning debut novel.... Utterly brilliant. Whoever you are, C. S., and whatever inside your head takes you to such dark places, go there again, and again. You're good." ***WINNIPEG FREE PRESS***

"A tough, carefully constructed mystery with a great setti and a great female detective. In short, for a debut, it's a winner and deserving of attention.... With a solid story..

just hope [C. S. Porter has] another Kes Morris book in the works." **THE GLOBE AND MAIL**

"C. S. Porter is a pseudonym for an exceptionally imaginative Canadian crime writer who sets their story in an unnamed rural area of the Maritimes.... [Kes is] a marvellous character, in theory open to friendship, but deliberately solitary, not allowing anyone to 'crack through the tough façade that lets her do her job.' And a heck of an inspired job it is."
TORONTO STAR

"Fast-paced and thought-provoking.... *Beneath Her Skin* is billed as a debut novel [but] it reads more like an offering from an author at their peak.... What is absolutely certain, as one is swept into this delicious, moving, completely satisfying gem of a noir detective novel, is they are not a rookie writer. Skillfully carrying the reader along as fast as a riptide, this novel is superbly paced, polished to perfection, and leaves the reader breathless for the next in this series."
THE MIRAMICHI READER

"A twisty, taut murder mystery.... I was struck by its economical prose, breakneck pace and intricate plot. With Kes, Porter has created a fallible yet fascinating enigmatic character... who deserves a series, or at least a second novel." ***ZOOMER, ZED BOOK CLUB PICK***

"The writing is first-rate, the novel tightly plotted. The reader is swept along by the expert pacing and the mounting suspense. Who is killing these people and why? As Kes digs into the town's history, she uncovers horrific secrets in the town's dark past." ***49TH SHELF***

"An excellent book, with well-paced and well considered characters. You can't go wrong with this one."
MURDER IN COMMON

SALT ON HER TONGUE

C. S. PORTER

A KES MORRIS FILE

Copyright © C. S. Porter, 2025

All rights reserved. No part of this book may be reproduced, stored in a retrieval system or transmitted in any form or by any means without the prior written permission from the publisher, or, in the case of photocopying or other reprographic copying, permission from Access Copyright, 1 Yonge Street, Suite 1900, Toronto, Ontario M5E 1E5.

Vagrant Press is an imprint of
Nimbus Publishing Limited
3660 Strawberry Hill Street, Halifax, NS, B3K 5A9
(902) 455-4286 nimbus.ca

Nimbus Publishing is based in Kjipuktuk, Mi'kma'ki, the traditional territory of the Mi'kmaq People.

Printed and bound in Canada
NB1759

Editor: Whitney Moran
Design: Jenn Embree

No part of this book may be used in the training of generative artificial intelligence technologies or systems.

This story is a work of fiction. Names, characters, incidents, and places, including organizations and institutions, are used fictitiously.

Library and Archives Canada Cataloguing in Publication

Title: Salt on her tongue : a Kes Morris file / C.S. Porter.
Names: Porter, C. S. (Author of Beneath her skin), author.
Identifiers: Canadiana (print) 20240512006 | Canadiana (ebook) 20240521862 | ISBN 9781774713624 (softcover) | ISBN 9781774713679 (EPUB)
Subjects: LCGFT: Detective and mystery fiction. | LCGFT: Novels.
Classification: LCC PS8631.O733 S25 2025 | DDC C813/.6—dc23

Nimbus Publishing acknowledges the financial support for its publishing activities from the Government of Canada, the Canada Council for the Arts, and from the Province of Nova Scotia. We are pleased to work in partnership with the Province of Nova Scotia to develop and promote our creative industries for the benefit of all Nova Scotians.

THE KES MORRIS SERIES

Beneath Her Skin
Salt on Her Tongue

PROLOGUE

Molly kicked the motel door shut behind them and pulled out the bottle of white wine she'd stolen from the restaurant. She peered through the bottle's neck, raising it until the liquid aligned with her eye, and rocked it back and forth, enjoying the effect. "You look like you're drowning."

Lucas switched on the lamp beside the bed. "Where did you get that?"

"The waitress gave it to me." Molly winked and pulled a foldable corkscrew from her pocket. "And this to go with it!" She snapped her fingers. "Cups, bathroom."

It made him nervous, the risks she took. He expected one day she'd get caught and wondered what would happen to him when she did. But it was that same playfulness and fearlessness that attracted him. He hadn't known Molly for long and she was careful with what she shared, always diverting their conversations away from herself. They were young and having fun and he was okay with that. He grabbed the plastic cups and glanced to the mirror and checked his teeth. He was a little drunk.

"The rule is, Luke, that we have to be naked when we drink this sucker." She opened the bottle and stripped right there in front of him while she poured wine into the cups. "How's that for balance?"

"It's...you're...beautiful." Lucas quickly pulled off his clothes. He could hardly believe she had chosen him over a dozen other guys peacocking around her in that bar. He reached for his cup. Molly lifted it above her head and looked down at his feet. He yanked off his socks and she handed him the drink. "Stay there."

She turned on the other bedside lamp, then switched on the harsh overhead light. She walked nude across the room, completely uninhibited, while he strained to keep his back straight and muscles taut. She opened the curtains looking out over the motel parking lot, and returned to stand in front of him. She grabbed the back of his neck, squeezed hard, then trailed her hand over his shoulder and down his torso, her fingertips settling just below his beltline.

With the other hand, she held her cup to his. "Cheers," she whispered in his ear. A hot shiver tingled down his neck. They downed their wine. She filled the glasses again then stepped aside and he shyly turned away from the window.

"Uh-uh." She positioned him to face the window. "Stay." She stepped behind him.

Lucas could see himself in the window's reflection. Exposed and erect. He scanned the parking lot for passersby or a car pulling in as she kissed his neck and her hands slid around his waist.

"Stay still," she whispered, and after that he didn't care who could see them.

I.

Kes had just returned from her tae kwon do class at Grand Master Jin's. The dojang was at the top of Radium Hill and with the exception of scheduled deliveries, Master Jin refused to allow cars up his drive.

In that broken time, when she had reached the bottom of herself and all she could do was run, Kes had made the pilgrimage up that tortuous hill every morning for over a month to arrive at five, before the sun had risen. He'd ask her why she was there and with every answer, he'd shut the door. Until finally, on the forty-eighth day, she confessed, near tears, "I don't know." And he let her in.

Master Jin was in his seventies and Kes was to be his last student, an immense honour. She had first found him after the Holy Cross case, when she couldn't shed the skin of something feral and empty still bristling in her blood. Mason would come to her in her dreams, wanting her to follow him. She would wake in terror, because she wanted to go with him. Master Jin was tough, but she grew to love and respect him. Three times a week, she trained under him. She began to feel her body, her breath, her power again. He had saved her, when she didn't know how to save herself. And then she left, when she thought she didn't need him anymore. She carried on with work, like she always did. Until he opened the door again.

She untied her black belt, 3rd Dan, and carefully rolled it up. It represented three hundred and sixty hours of practice and techniques she saw in her sleep now: front leg roundhouse kick, jump front leg side kick, inside out crescent kick—kick (*chagi*), block (*makgi*), strike (*chigi*)—tiger claw, eagle strike, pincer-hand... the latter always reminded her of lobsters. She laid the belt in her dresser drawer alongside the perfect coils of whites, yellows, greens, blues, and reds, representing birth, strength, growth, confidence, caution; and black, the combination of all. Signifying the darkness beyond the sun, the perpetual search for knowledge and self—impervious to fear.

Kes didn't know if she could ever achieve the latter. Fear kept her safe. It reminded her to keep coming back from the edge. Soon she hoped to achieve her 4th degree black belt, if her master thought she was ready. She didn't tell Master Jin why she had missed her lessons when she was sick of heart and body. He hadn't asked. Their relationship wasn't based in words.

Kes pulled off her sweat-soaked dobok, brushed away a smudge of dust at the cuff, and set it aside to wash. She recited the tenets in her mind: *courtesy, integrity, perseverance, self-control, indomitable spirit.*

Her phone rang. Her work ringtone. Shrill and loud. A sound she hadn't heard in weeks. She grabbed her cell from the window ledge.

"Kes Morris." Her voice was hoarse from lack of use.

"Detective. Captain Francis here. I have a job I want you to do for me."

"You put me on medical leave, sir."

"They say you're clean. You've been cleared to return to unrestricted duty."

"Yes, sir." Six months, twenty-eight days, six hours since she came back from hell. Counting every minute to this call.

"Unless you're not ready." He had access to all of her progress reports and psych evaluations. She had done the work. Done everything they had asked of her. Told them what they needed to hear.

"I'm ready."

"Good. This is a discretionary assignment. You understand?"

"Yes, sir."

"Be in my office in an hour." The line went dead.

Kes hung up and realized she was standing in front of the open window in just her underwear and bra. She sensed she was being watched. She checked the neighbours' windows. Her eyes sharpened. Not a movement. Not a shadow. She breathed in the cool air of dying vegetation and dry earth. Heard only the soft sound of cars up the road, the rustle of fall leaves, and the close caw of a crow. The bird called again and she saw it, not a crow but a raven, high in a tree, black against the yellowing foliage, watching her. It bobbed its head and flew. She headed to the shower and just for a moment, she checked in with herself: "Are you ready?"

In an instant, she was back in that green room with the fluorescent light, curled up, bathed in sweat, shaking, muscles cramping, the tortured craving...the smell of pain and poison seeping from her pores. A failed drug test. Three weeks in rehab. Not enough. Four months' extended medical leave to keep a suspension off the books. Two months of accumulated vacation and sick days to give her more time. Forty-eight runs up the hill to Master Jin's, twelve thousand four hundred and twenty-eight steps. A thousand shames. The cost of those little white pills. She centred herself—*I'm not there anymore, I'm not her anymore*—and turned on the water.

She was Detective Kes Morris.

II.

Kes took the elevator up to the sixth floor of the new police department. It was one of the best architectural designs in the city, but she thought the interior was totally inappropriate for a working police station. All fresh and lively, a modern style that already felt scuffed and torn—and she didn't know a single cop who liked pastels. She walked down the hall to the captain's corner office and tugged at the tails of her shirt before knocking.

She didn't know Captain Francis well; he was brought in from the outside not long before he put her on leave. She knew he was an ambitious man who commanded a great deal of respect within the department. Among the men at least. Most of the woman found him arrogant and condescending. He had taken all the mandatory human resource classes—hadn't they all—but that hadn't softened his disposition. He was a good, no-nonsense captain, she'd give him that, but she missed her old captain. He had been one of the few who could read her and gave her the leeway to do her job. She heard he'd retired to Portugal. Kes had never seen him with a tan.

Captain Francis's office was glass-walled. He could be seen and he could watch. His right hand, Lucy, was stationed outside his door overseeing paperwork and phones. She stopped Kes as she walked past her desk. "Excuse me, do you have an appointment, Detective?"

"Yes," Kes indulged the gatekeeper, though the captain could see her.

"One moment." Lucy reached for her phone to announce Kes's arrival, and Captain Francis waved her in.

"Afternoon, Captain."

"Ah, Morris. Right on time. Have a seat, this won't take long." He glanced up from his paperwork and gave her a sample of his winning smile. "Be right with you."

There were rumours he had higher political aspirations. She didn't envy him being the face of public apologies and protecting the blue line, hollow words that always sounded rehearsed.

Kes took a seat across from him. The office was sterile and devoid of any personal items. Instead, the only shelved wall behind the desk held awards and photos of Captain Francis with important people. Politicians mostly. The glass and the sleek furnishings gleamed with a showroom polish. Artificial and anonymous. She glanced out the windows towards the harbour. Two tugboats were leading a cargo ship under the bridge. She remembered her father telling her the tugboat's design was the same in harbours all around the world. *Workhorse of the ocean,* he'd say. Functionality, he'd believed, was beauty in its own way.

"I'm sending you on a missing persons case, Morris. A young woman disappeared yesterday up in Spectacle Harbour. Boyfriend reported her missing."

"I don't investigate missing persons..." She quickly added, "sir." But it sounded tagged on. And it was. The captain looked up and leaned back in his chair.

"The missing girl is a senator's daughter."

Did he really think he was doing her a favour,

sending her on a case to win him brownie points with a politician?

"That's not what I do. Sir."

Captain Francis sat up straighter and crossed his arms, closing off any further discussion. "Detective Morris, this is an opportunity for you to ease back in. A test case, if you will. I think you're capable of making a few inquiries without drawing attention. A quiet case that I expect you to close quickly and discreetly. When you find her, tell the young woman to call her father." He slid a slim file across the table. "She was last seen in Spectacle Harbour. The local precinct in Hawthorne's Junction is expecting you and has agreed to offer you every courtesy. You'll report back to me, and only to me."

Kes opened the folder and saw a photo of a young woman, twenty-two years old, 5'8", dark shoulder-length hair, careful makeup, olive complexion, blue eyes. Hard in their intensity. Thin, forced smile, staring at the camera. Head tilted, chin up...defiant? Seated in a park? A backyard? Kes looked over the one-page report, a sparse statement from the boyfriend, a Lucas Knox, twenty-one. The young man had left her for thirty minutes and she'd disappeared.

"So this girl ditched her boyfriend and that's the basis for calling me in? It hasn't even been twenty-four hours, how does"—she checked the name—"Molly Kinder qualify as missing?" She knew the answer: it wasn't about the girl; it was about who her father was.

"This is a favour to me," the captain said.

So this was how he was going to play it, she thought. He had kept her record clean and now she owed him. He was her enemy, not her ally. "And then I'm back to my full duties?" Quid pro quo.

"If this goes well," he said, "I don't see why not."

Integrity, a core tenet. She looked to the captain's clean-shaven cheeks and crisp collar. She imagined he had a razor and multiple identical pressed shirts in his private bathroom. There was nothing amiss on him. He was perfectly buttoned up. Just once, she vowed, she would play the game to get back to what she did best. She would make this one concession.

"Anything else I should know about this young woman? Any activity on her accounts or phone?"

"No, and she wasn't carrying a phone." He tapped the desk twice with his fingers like Kes was taking up his precious time.

She didn't bother asking how he had access to that information already. "History of running away, mental illness, family issues...?"

"You have what I know."

She held his eyes, waiting for a tell. The captain smiled and she thought, *There it is.*

"Lucy has booked you a room at the Orchard Way Motel. I hear it's pretty up there. She also has a car for you."

"No car necessary. I always use my own. It's how I work." This was non-negotiable. Her father came with her. "I accept the risk that it isn't insured."

He eyed her curiously, as though considering whether arguing this point was worth his time. "As long as that is fully understood." He returned to his paperwork and with that, she was dismissed. She gathered up the thin file and headed for the door.

"It's good to have you back, Detective Morris."

She didn't trust his words. He had shown himself. There were conditions to his forgiveness.

"Thank you, sir." She felt the stickiness of shame on her tongue.

"Next time, though, Detective"—he looked up—"if you cross the line, there won't be a free pass."

"Yes, sir."

III.

On the drive to Spectacle Harbour, Kes realized she would have to call Bjorn to cancel their date tonight. They had been seeing each other for a few weeks now, ever since they literally ran into one another at Ocean Park along the North trail when she was making her final sprint for the parking lot. He had recently arrived from Copenhagen to teach ethics at the city university and was one of the most beautiful men Kes had ever seen. The moment she saw him, she wanted him. A deep, primal desire. The first she had felt since her divorce. Purely animal. The fact that he was smart, kind, interesting, and strangely calming was disarming. She would have to think of an excuse as to why she was going out of town. She had withheld from him that she was a homicide detective. How was that for ethics and integrity?

In her defense, when she was with him she just wanted to be a normal person, to see her city through the eyes of a newcomer and have easy chats about ordinary life. She wanted to be who she might have been, unjaded by all the atrocities she had witnessed. And it felt good to not be her, for a little while. But being on the road again felt even better.

Soon she left behind the double-laned highway and opted for the old route to the coast. It was slower and a little longer, but the Jaguar loved the winding road.

The tighter the curves, the more it steadied to the challenge. It was the perfect ride through the countryside on a beautiful mid-September afternoon. Crisp air, pale sunlight, the maple and birch just beginning to turn colour. She could almost forget she was on a case. If she could call it that.

It was almost two hours before she began the long, steep climb that led to the Bay of Fundy. A male pheasant flushed across the road in front of her, flying so low she would have struck it if she hadn't slammed on the brakes. Her tires squealed, leaving burn marks on the pavement, and the bird glided into the woods and vanished. Stupid, beautiful bird. She was thankful it had been spared.

She pulled over at the top of the hill, or "mountain" as the locals called it, and stepped out of the car to take in the breathtaking view. There was a thin wash of fog floating above the bay, like something a pastry chef might add to a confection. On the far side, she could just make out the thin line of the other coast wrapping around the bay. Though only twenty miles across, it would take almost two hours to drive around. The water was a deep blue-black and even from this distance Kes could tell it was moving swiftly, churning with the region's notoriously massive tides.

Kes remembered learning about the tidal bore in high school. In a single day, more water flowed in and out of the bay than through all the rivers of the world combined. Over a period of six hours it would rise from sea level to fifty feet, then drop six hours later. The ocean breathing. A constant ebb and flow that carved away towering red cliffs. It held whales in its depths. Yet, a few hours later a boat could run aground. It had always awed Kes. The improbability. The force. The uniqueness and mystery of this place.

She scanned the horizon, trying to confirm if she was seeing the far western shore or the neighbouring province from this vantage point. It was so easy to get disoriented. Clouds looked like land. Land disappeared in mirages of light. This area was once attached to Africa and the separation of continents had created the Atlantic and this bay. Just standing here looking down at it was a powerful experience. She would have to tell Olivia about this place. Maybe they could come back together someday and look for fossils.

Kes leaned against the hood of the Jag and felt the heat rising from the engine. The air was cooler up here and smelled of mud and brine and lingering depths. The trees were getting scrubbier and some leaves were already red. She wasn't in any rush to leave this beauty behind. She hoped she'd find the girl quickly and maybe take a few days to roam and explore, let herself get lost. The weather was supposed to be perfect.

She got back in the car and looked to the file on her seat. She flipped it open and studied the girl's features and wondered how recent the photo was. She punched in the name on her phone and didn't any get any hits. She searched for the senator; there were plenty of images of him. *Smug* was the word that came to mind. She closed the file, put away her phone, and shifted into first.

Another fifteen minutes and she was making the descent to the bay. The coastal road was in dire need of paving and soon the frost would be heaving beneath it again. She passed an old farmstead. Two draft horses strolled along the fenceline. On the ocean side was a cluster of small cottages. In front of one, a large man in a speedo was mowing his lawn.

She reached the exit for Spectacle Harbour and turned off. She was surprised to see two huge government wharves and an impressively constructed breakwater protecting them. A lot of government money had been invested here. The road leading down was freshly paved and the dock was lined with lamp posts, electrical outlets, and cleats for the boats to tie off to. She had counted only forty-two houses dotting the rocky land.

A cluster of brightly painted fish shacks huddled at the head of one of the wharves. They looked as though they had been painted by women's hands. Cheerful bright pinks, purples, blues, reds, and doors embellished with hand-drawn flowers. Wives, daughters, girlfriends? These reminders of home were odd and lovely amidst the working dock.

Brand new pickup trucks were parked at the head of the piers and men—it appeared to be all men—were busy prepping and loading lobster traps and provisions onto the waiting vessels. No one seemed to take notice of the old green Jag parked at the turnaround. Kes watched them busy with their chores on deck, as others slung gear over their shoulders and climbed down the ten-foot metal-rung ladders to the flat-bottomed fishing boats. She glanced to the impossible high-water mark on the wharf above them and the depth still to drain from the basin. She wasn't sure if the tide was rising or falling.

She looked around the small protected harbour and wondered if the missing girl had come this way. Maybe walked down to the wharf? Across the road was a fish plant. All the community's buildings looked out over the harbour. Molly, a city girl, would have been noticed wandering around here. It wasn't a tourist spot. There weren't any pleasure boats in the harbour; this was a working dock and every berth was filled.

Kes watched a young man cutting herring for bait. Beside him were hundreds of stacked traps with buoy lines neatly coiled inside. He impaled the chum on a metal spike and set it in a trap. Brazen seagulls, waiting for an opportunity to snatch a treat, grew impatient and lifted in a complaint of squawks before settling again in the same spot. Another crew member grabbed the baited trap and lowered it to a boat, where a deckhand tightly stacked it at the stern. An older man, the captain likely, checked every trap, adjusted lines, and supervised placement. Everything smelled of fish and sea.

Kes typed in her location and *tide* on her phone. No signal. She would need to pick up a chart to determine when boats could have sailed in and out. She felt someone watching her and looked to the fish plant. A woman in the middle top-floor window turned away. Kes made a note to visit the woman after she spoke to the missing girl's boyfriend and checked into the motel.

A truck pulled out from the loading bay around the back of the plant. A stream of ice water ran through a gap in the back doors. Kes's first impression of Spectacle Harbour was that of a typical small port on a scenic coast preparing for fishing season. A place where days came and went like the tide.

IV.

THE NEAREST DETACHMENT WAS TEN MINUTES INLAND IN Hawthorn's Junction, a village that had seen better times. It seemed to comprise mostly weathered wooden homes and neglected brick or stone buildings, many of them empty. The façades still bore the names of a post office, banks, and various merchants. It had once been a booming place.

Kes parked in the visitor's section at the front of a pinkish stone building. *Granite maybe? Or sandstone from a local quarry?* A worn plaque dated the building to 1806. Based on the signage, the police evidently shared the structure with the town archives. It was surprising there was still a small precinct with an advisory board here at all; most had been consolidated and handed over to the RCMP, but this village had held on to theirs.

Upon entering, Kes found herself in a reception area. The woman at the veneer desk didn't look up from her crossword puzzle until she completed writing in 5 across: *S-E-A-S-O-N-E-D*. Beside her was a mug with *SANDY* in bold cursive letters. Kes studied the woman's bowed head. Harsh blond, the roots long and grey. Her nails were clipped short and she smelled like lilac. Her sweater had the looseness of years of washing. There wasn't a pill in the wool. Kes wondered how she kept it so pristine, thinking of all the sweaters she had thrown out over the years.

She scanned the woman's crossword clues and empty boxes and filled in the answers in her head—*gnu, Paraguay, gymnastic, Nureyev, unruly*—and noted the error at 17 down. The woman, presumably Sandy, stuck her pencil behind her ear and covered the puzzle with her hands, as though they had just come to casually rest there.

"Help you?"

"This is the police station?"

"Obviously."

"I'm here to speak to a young man I'm told you're holding."

"Name?"

"Kes Morris."

"We don't have anyone by that name."

"No, that's me. I'm here to see Lucas..." Kes reached in her pocket for her notepad and flipped open the first page, irritated that his name had escaped her. She took a breath; it was her first day back on the job, *be easy on yourself.*

"When you find out, come back."

Kes's hackles raised. "OK, let's start again. I'm..."

Sandy looked past Kes to the man entering and beamed. "Hi, Bert."

"Hey, Sandy. Everything all right here?" The man was wearing a worn coat with patched elbows. He was a tall, large man who carried his weight easily, and had a slouch to his shoulders that made his size seem less intimidating. He could be a fisherman. Definitely a local. Kes could smell the salt air on him.

"Under control," Sandy confirmed.

The man casually nodded to Kes, as though acknowledging a tourist in town, but then paused as if trying to place her. He smiled and stuck out his hand. "Detective Kes Morris? Bert Hawthorn, Chief. We finally meet, I've heard so much about you."

He shuffled out of his worn coat and pulled on his police jacket, which had been hanging on a hook by the door. "So good to have you here. Come with me. Sandy, bring us a pot of tea, won't you? And that nice cup for the detective."

"Of course." Sandy's graciousness evaporated the moment the chief passed by her desk. Her lips tightened and her eyes emptied as Kes followed Hawthorn into his office. Kes had no idea what she had done to piss this woman off.

Hawthorn's office was a shabby wood-panelled affair with a high ceiling and ornate window that overlooked a small park. Outside, a young boy was smashing a stick against a metal swing set while his mother chatted away on her cellphone. The deep, hollow thunk resonated discordantly.

Kes focused on an antique double-barrelled shotgun hanging behind the desk and a pair of vintage fly-fishing rods propped in the corner.

The chief emptied his pockets into his desk drawer. Kes recognized the rituals of switching from off-duty to on. "The kid, Lucas, has been here all night. Checked out of the motel yesterday morning. Apparently only had enough money for one night. Says he used up all his savings for the big date. We tried to send him back to the city but he refused, thinking his girlfriend might come back."

Bert sat down heavily in the old oak banker's chair and wheeled it back to give himself more berth from the table. "We let him stay in lock-up overnight; nobody was using it and you were coming up today...I figured you might want to talk to him."

"Do you think he's complicit in Molly Kinder's disappearance, sir?"

"Heard you like to get right to the point, Detective." He had a big, easy smile and his demeanour suggested he was rarely riled. "Nope, I don't."

"Why not?"

"You are in a hurry, Detective." His invitation for her to take a seat.

The chair was uncomfortable, stiff-backed and low, which made Kes have to look up to him. "Why don't you think he's involved?"

"Well, there were no signs of struggle. No marks on the boy."

"That doesn't eliminate him as a suspect."

"No, but I spoke to him personally and I believe his story."

"That she just disappeared?" Kes didn't mask her skepticism.

"Maybe she left." Hawthorn's voice tightened and his back straightened. A small shift, but Kes surmised he didn't like being questioned on his own turf and was unaccustomed to having his authority challenged.

"And why would she do that?"

"That's your job, Detective. Or so I'm told." He smiled, but his eyes didn't.

Kes knew she was coming on too strong and he was letting her know. *Patience,* she reminded herself. She tried softening her tone. "Sorry, Chief, I'm usually called in after the missing person is found." A weak attempt that fell flat.

"I understand this is a special circumstance, Detective. We don't usually get someone like you sent to our little bay. Someone must have some pull, beyond you and I, to prioritize this case. If it *is* a case. Calling in the big dog, not even twenty-four hours in."

They agreed on that. The chief had a manner that put one at ease and a calm demeanour that suggested things were going to work out, but she knew he was observing her as closely as she was him.

"What do we have so far, sir?"

"A pretty young lady vanished in minutes, according to the boy. Lucas..." He checked his notes for the last name.

"Knox." Kes wouldn't forget again.

"Far as I can tell, two kids came out here for an adventure and I'm guessing one of them bailed."

"How? Did she have a car? Hitch a ride? And where did she go? She hasn't used her bank cards, no withdrawals, no calls. Is there a taxi company out here?"

The captain laughed. "No, ma'am."

"Abducted?"

"Sure doubt that."

Kes's shoulders tensed. The chief's lax approach was starting to irritate her. This was the job, even if it turned out to be a bored rich kid on the lam. She expected professionalism. *Patience. Patience.*

"And why aren't we looking at that as an option, Chief?"

"Of all the harbours along the bay, Spectacle is the quietest. The most 'Christian.' Old families who have known each another for years. Rarely a dispute. Not like Niels Cove. Or Crooked Bay. I've been chief here for near twenty years now and we've never had a serious crime, and I can count the petty ones in the low dozens. Most differences here can be talked out. I pride myself on that."

"What about the harbour? Is that as quiet? Boats come in from elsewhere. A lot can happen in secluded harbours. I've worked in small towns."

"Anything that comes in or goes out gets seen, Detective. You can't just sail in. It's a small window along this coast. You go by the tide. It dictates everything. Always has."

"Where does the tide stand now, sir?"

"Running out." He didn't even have to check.

She jotted down a note. "And yesterday morning, when the missing person was last seen?"

"Would have been high tide."

"How deep is Spectacle Harbour at high tide?"

"Twenty-five feet."

"It must have quite the pull."

"It surely does."

Kes stood. "I'd like to talk to Lucas now, sir."

"No tea?" The chief seemed bemused by her eagerness. "You'll find time makes its own pace here, Detective. You'll feel the rhythm soon. You can't help it. We're more water than blood."

Sandy arrived with a cup of tea in a floral cup and a handful of creamers and sugar.

"Ah, thank you, Sandy, but the detective's going to skip the tea."

Chief Hawthorne got up from his desk and led the way. "I'll show you where to find our young man. I'll take that cuppa, Sandy. You can leave it on my desk."

As Kes passed Sandy, she attempted conciliation. "Thanks for that, maybe next time."

"Next time, I'll show you where the kettle is," Sandy replied. "Tea bags right beside it."

Kes was making friends fast in this town. If she could locate the girl, maybe she could be back in time for a late dinner with Bjorn. She would like that.

V.

Kes followed Hawthorn down the hall. Their steps echoed off the hardwood floor and bounced off the high ceiling. He had a habit of walking with his weight on his heels. He probably had back issues.

"Cells are at the end of this corridor. I presume you don't need me for this?" He didn't wait for her to answer. "Keep me posted on any developments or if we can assist, but word from above is it's all yours now. Good to meet you, Detective Morris. It's not every day we get to see a big-city detective at work."

It felt like a jab, but his eyes were friendly and she didn't sense any animosity.

"Thank you, Chief. Hopefully I'll be out of your way soon."

"Or maybe this place will grab hold of you, like it does most, and you won't want to leave. Good luck, Detective."

Kes waited for his heavy footsteps to recede. Approaching the cell she could hear faint music, as if muffled through headphones. Something fast and loud. She rounded the corner and saw the open cage, a backpack, a bag of chips, a carton of milk, and a sneakered foot keeping beat. She was in the cell before he noticed her. He was young, and university hip. He had a light build. 5'10." Clean-cut. Urban. Trendy hair.

He yanked out his earbuds and shut off his phone. There were dark bags under his eyes. Likely hadn't slept.

"Hi, Lucas. I'm Detective Morris."

"Is there any news? Has anyone seen her? I've been telling them she wouldn't just take off." He was speaking quickly, like he was truly concerned. His breathing was fast and his cheeks flushed. His heart rate was up. "We were having a good time. At least I thought we were. I was only gone a—"

Kes stopped him. "Let's go for a stroll, Lucas. It's hot in here. You can tell me about the last time you saw Molly. I find I think better in the light. That good for you?" She wanted him to settle before she talked to him. Make him feel comfortable with her.

The young man shoved his phone and earbuds into his backpack. His hands were shaking and his underarms were sweat stained. He seemed younger than his age. Awkward. Not the kind of boy you'd expect would catch the attention of a wealthy, "pretty" girl.

"I think it's safe to leave your gear here," she said.

"I've never talked to a detective before." He was nervous. But she could have that effect on the innocent, too.

"We're just going to have a conversation."

The ground around the picnic table was littered with cigarette butts and a spattering of fallen maple leaves. Lucas picked up a nut from the ground. "Acorn," he said like he had found something lucky. An innocent distraction? A lapse in his performance?

Kes corrected him. "Chestnut, I think."

She watched him roll the nut back and forth in his hand. His hands hadn't seen hard labour. There were no cuts or scratches to indicate a physical altercation. He looked up as a red-winged blackbird settled on a branch of the giant chestnut tree, its leaves just starting to brown.

"It's a beautiful bird," Kes said. "That flash of crimson on its wing sets it apart from the other black birds." And for a few moments they just watched it. Lucas's hands stopped trembling.

"I've never seen one before," he said softly.

"You're a student?"

"Third year."

She watched his body calm. A quiet conversation, nothing more. "What are you studying?"

"Urban planning."

"And Molly?"

His shoulders tightened at the mention of her name. "General arts. She said she was only there because her father insisted on a 'proper' degree and it was his money. But she's smart. I think most of her classes bored her."

"How did you meet?"

"At school. At the student union bar." He set the chestnut on the table. "We hit it off."

She wondered if they had. He didn't sound convinced. "How long ago was that?"

"Few weeks ago. We've been hanging out since then. She didn't have a car and if she needed to go somewhere, I took her. She'd wait outside class for me or come to my dorm."

"Did you ever go to her dorm?"

"Yeah."

"Is that allowed?"

He hesitated. "Not really. They have floor monitors who keep an eye out for anyone who doesn't live there."

"How did you get around that?" Kes pretended to be impressed.

"When the coast was clear she'd sit on a bench at the base of this bronze horse statue out front. That was her signal."

"How did you end up here?"

"We wanted to get away before midterms."

"Whose idea was it to come?"

"Hers. She said she'd never been to the Bay of Fundy, so..."

"So you booked a motel."

"Yeah. She's a photographer. Always taking pictures. That's what we were going to do yesterday. Walk around, see what she could find."

"So what happened? Walk me through your morning, just so I can picture it. Take your time." Kes casually pulled out her notepad. Lucas didn't balk, she had his trust.

"We got up really early. She wanted first light and we knew the boats would be getting ready. They told us at the motel, the fishing season's about to open. We dropped off the key and drove down to the wharf. It was still pretty dark and it was cold. There was dew on the grass and windshield." His nails were chewed short and he had a habit of rubbing his fingers over the jagged tips for comfort or reassurance. He spoke with his head down, staring at the chestnut.

"When we came up the rise, the sun was just coming up and the sky lit up red. The tide was in." He looked up, like he was seeing it again. "I stopped, so she could take some pictures, and then we headed down to the wharves. I couldn't park too close 'cause of all the trucks.

It was real busy. So I pulled over and she got out, but then she said she forgot her camera charger in the room. She didn't want to miss the light and asked if I would go back for it."

He glanced to Kes, but couldn't hold eye contact. *Guilt? Shame?* He looked away and his hand went to his mouth and he surreptitiously chewed on his thumbnail before dropping it self-consciously. He slipped his hands under his thighs. Kes knew he had been reprimanded in the past for chewing his nails.

"So you went back to the motel?"

"Yeah, I had to get the key again, but the charger wasn't there. It must have been in her bag and she forgot or didn't see it. I wasn't gone half an hour. When I got back the sun was up and I could see right across the bay, but I couldn't find her."

His eyes were darting like he was scanning the water. Reliving the moment. "I went up and down the wharves asking everyone, but no one had seen her. I checked the shoreline in both directions, but the tide was high and there was barely any beach left. I thought maybe she'd gone looking for a photo and something happened."

"Then what did you do?"

Her question startled him. He blinked back the memories. "I drove up to the houses and around the buildings, I came back and stopped on the rise. You can see everything from up there. But I couldn't see Molly anywhere. I went back to the motel, thinking she might show up, then I came here to report her missing. I looked. I really looked. How can someone just be gone?" His voice quavered, like a child trying not to cry.

Kes agreed with Hawthorn. Lucas was just a scared kid whose friend had vanished. He wasn't involved in Molly's disappearance.

"Did you call her cell?"

"She doesn't have one. She calls them 'leashes.' She never wanted to be on a leash."

"Did she have a bag or suitcase?"

"Just her shoulder bag. She had it with her."

Kes jotted down a note. "Was your relationship intimate, Lucas? Were you more than friends?"

His ears reddened. "Does that matter?"

Kes already had her answer. "You were the last known person to see Molly, so I'm trying to understand her state of mind at the time of her disappearance."

"She was fine. We were having fun. She was different, you know?"

"What do you mean by that?"

"She was confident...made her own rules. A bit wild. Sort of made me feel like I was old-fashioned. She wasn't self-conscious or afraid of anything." He averted his eyes. Embarrassed to be talking about sex.

"Is it possible she just took off? Hitched her way home?"

He looked at her, absolute in his conviction. "Molly wouldn't just leave like that. Who would do that?"

Kes closed her notepad. "You've been very helpful, Lucas. Chief Hawthorn has your contact information. If we have any other questions, someone will be in touch."

"That's it?"

Kes slipped her notepad back into her pocket. "This is where we start."

"What am I supposed to do?" He sounded exhausted.

"Go home," she said gently.

"You're going to find her, right? You'll let me know?"

She couldn't make any promises. Besides, it didn't work that way. He wasn't next of kin. He was a new boyfriend who had little history with the possible victim. He probably didn't even know her middle name.

"You don't think something bad happened to her, do you?"

She handed him her card. "If you think of anything else, you can call me."

Kes left Lucas at the bench and headed to the parking lot. The small boy who'd been hitting trees with the stick was tightrope walking the curb and taking imaginary swings at cars. His mother was still on her phone. Kes's Jag was the next in line to be threatened. She walked up to her car. The boy froze in her presence, a stranger. He guiltily dropped the stick to his side.

Kes stared at the little boy, noting the stained T-shirt and grubby sneakers. He was just bored and lonely. Seeking attention, no matter the consequence. "Hi," she said, looking down at him. "Are you keeping guard so nothing happens to these cars?"

He looked uncertain, knowing that wasn't his intention at all. He nodded a lie. She reached in her pocket for her keys and let her coat part so he could see her badge. The little boy stared hard at it and back up at her.

"You're doing a great job. I sure would be upset if someone hurt my car, like if someone broke your favourite toy on purpose. That wouldn't feel good, would it?" He shook his head. She smiled. "Thank you, for protecting my toy."

She got in the car and revved the engine for the boy's pleasure. She checked the rear-view as she pulled away. The boy had picked up the stick again, but was now standing guard, warding off imaginary threats from the woods. His mother was still on the phone. Kes stopped and rolled down her window. She counted to twenty-seven before the woman looked up.

"Is that your son?" Kes asked.

The woman looked to the boy and back to Kes, confused and wary. "Why?" Her tone made it clear she was accustomed to defending him.

"You have no friggin' idea how lucky you are and you're ignoring him. There won't be many more days like this. Someday you might regret that."

Kes slowly pulled away. She had broken two of her discipline's guiding principles, *courtesy* and *self-control*. It was worth it.

VI.

Kes drove back towards the harbour. She pulled over at the look-off. Phone reception was better up here, but her call went straight to voice mail.

"Bjorn. Hi, it's Kes. Sorry but I won't be able to meet you tonight. Bit of a last-minute work thing. I really wanted to see you..." She sounded like a schoolgirl. *Stay light and casual, no expectations*, she chided herself. "I'll call when I get back to town."

She hung up and breathed in. What the hell was she doing? Did she really want a man in her life at this point? Was he just an escape? How fair was that to him? But the sex. It was like a hunger. Just being near him felt electric. Didn't she deserve some happiness? She took in the view and let the expanse wash over her. This basin was emptying and farther up the narrows it had already receded, leaving a wide, mud-red swath.

She tried to imagine the bay when it was filled with schooners darting from cove to cove. Up and down the coast, the wooden remains of shipbuilding docks jutted like ribs from the sand. What would it have been like when Fagundes, de Mons, and Champlain first sailed in? Did the ebb and flow catch them by surprise? Did they have to make a rapid retreat before their ships grounded? Did they show any humility to the Indigenous people who'd lived here for centuries? And what did the

Mi'kmaq think when they first saw those white sails? And watched them drive crosses into the land's highest crags? Her mind was flooded with a torrent and she had to force it to slow. It was so much easier to manage with the pills. She counted the boats in the harbour and the birds on the powerlines and her mind calmed.

The sun was getting lower and the colours richer. She wished Bjorn was with her to see this place. She wished he had picked up the call. She looked down to Spectacle Harbour and got back in her car. The motel could wait. She'd check out the fish plant before it closed for the day. Work would keep Bjorn out of her head.

At the wharf, the men were packing up their kits and heading home for dinner. The boats were now settled on the basin's bottom, resting in muddy red shallow pools, not even ankle deep. Long slack spring lines stretched at forty-five-degree angles from the bow and stern up to the dock far above. *This is true low tide*, Kes noted.

She pulled in slowly. A few heads turned to take in the Jag, but didn't express any interest or surprise. She knew they were truck men; a vehicle like hers would be considered useless. She parked close to the fish plant, careful not to block the gravel road encircling the building.

There was a *DO NOT ENTER* sign at a side entrance, but Kes couldn't see another way in. She pushed open the heavy steel door and was surprised by how clean and bright it was inside. Long stainless-steel conveyers spanned the workspace, which extended much farther than she had assumed. A small forklift criss-crossed the back of the plant, dropping plastic crates at the end of each station with speed and precision.

"Wait till you see this place in a couple'a days," a voice boomed from above.

Kes looked up to a man standing on a second-floor walkway. He wore a pair of bib overalls and was jotting something on a metal clipboard.

"Why is that?" she asked.

"Be hundreds of pounds of lobsters on those belts you're looking at, and a full workforce grading, separating, packaging, or loading trucks. It's kinda nice when it's quiet like this. You're not supposed to be in here, but I'm guessin' you know that already."

"I hoped to ask a few questions about yesterday morning." She held up her badge. "I'm Detective—"

"I know who you are. Come on up. Stairs are right there." The man motioned towards the far wall and retreated into his office. He left the door open for her.

Kes didn't like heights and the metal staircase had open honeycomb steps that clanged with each footfall. She tried not to look down at the concrete floor beneath her.

The office overlooked both the plant inside and the harbour outside. It reminded Kes of a ship's bridge. The man was already seated at his desk, which faced a window overseeing the factory below. Behind him, at the other desk with the harbour view, was a woman entering numbers on an oversized calculator. It was the same woman Kes had seen watching her earlier. Their desks were piled high with paperwork. Neither looked up.

"Thanks for your time," Kes said. "I know you're busy."

"You have no idea. Give me a second." He searched through a stack of papers. "Gladdie, you seen the paperwork for the *Maudie*? What time's she due in?"

"Under your coffee cup: 2:15 A.M." The woman didn't look up from hand-scribing her calculations into a ledger. The office didn't have the order or cleanliness of the main floor. The desks, chairs, and lamps were worn and grimy. A stained, empty coffee pot was perched on a dented file cabinet. Document boxes were stacked in corners. One wall was crammed with corkboards layered with invoices and another an oversized marine chart. There was still a landline on the woman's desk and in the corner a vintage marine radio.

"What can I do you for?" The man laid down his paperwork.

"I didn't catch your name," Kes said. He had a strength to him and a surprising calm when he focused on her.

"I didn't tell you." His eyes smiled, but he didn't offer it.

She was willing to play for a little while. He was sussing her out, too. "Early yesterday morning, did you happen to notice a young woman down on the docks taking photographs?"

"Nope. I didn't get here until later." His cell rang. "Sorry, I got to take this. Gladdie, you see a young gal on the dock yesterday?" he called loudly as he stepped onto the gangway to take the call.

Gladdie turned her chair around, took off her reading glasses, and let them hang from the twine around her neck. Kes held her stare. Neither looked away. "Yeah, I saw her. She had a camera. Didn't see her taking any pictures, though. Saw you down there today, too."

Kes figured Gladdie saw most everything, and by the way she swatted the fly beside her, she doubted she was as deaf as her boss seemed to think.

"Did you see her get on one of the boats?"

"No way that's going to happen. Beginnin' of season. Too much work to get done to stop for sightseeing. Plus, there weren't no boats going out."

"Did you notice her get into a vehicle?"

"Nope."

"Any other boats around?"

Gladdie put down her stubbed pencil. "I'm not always looking out the window, you know."

A little too defensive. This woman was holding something back. "But you did see something…"

"One pass-by. Came in slowly by the far pier then sped off. There's no docking for pleasure boats around here."

Kes pulled out her notepad. "What kind of a boat?"

"Money—loud, useless. Made of good wood by the look of it. Mahogony, teak? Flash and brass. Probably out the yacht club on the other side of the bay."

"Out-of-province?" Kes looked out the window, tried to find her bearing, but the distant coastline had been swallowed by an encroaching fog bank. You wouldn't know there was land across the way.

"That'd be my guess."

"Can you reach the fishermen on that?" Kes nodded to the radio. "Ask if anyone noticed the girl or saw her get on that boat?"

"This time of day, couple might still be on their boats, but most are in their trucks heading home or picking up provisions. They start work a lot earlier…" She stopped short from saying "…than you," but Kes heard it nonetheless.

"If it wouldn't be too much trouble, I'd like you to try," Kes insisted.

Gladdie slipped on a huge pair of headphones,

adjusted the radio frequencies, and called into the handset asking if anyone had seen a girl taking pictures yesterday. She waited for an answer. "I know, I know." She laughed and glanced to Kes, who couldn't hear the response, but imagined the quip on the other end was at her expense.

Kes studied the bird's-eye map of the harbour, trying to get a sense of the coves and inlets. Her eyes followed the coastline that tapered inland to where the river met the ocean and tourists and locals rode the tidal bore on rafts and tire tubes. She continued following the curving coast around the basin and up along the opposite shore until she was directly across from Spectacle. A massive swath of undeveloped land, beyond her jurisdiction.

Gladdie pulled off the headphones. "One of the guys seems to remember her. Maybe she waved to the craft, maybe she was swatting a mosquito."

"Is there a boat that can take me out? I'd like to get a look from the water."

"It's almost Dumping Day." As if that was an answer. Gladdie called out to the man on the gangway. "Spruce!" He held up his hand, indicating he needed another second. Kes observed the man's palm, slashed with scars from hauling rope. "He's a busy man," Gladdie said, and nothing else.

Kes waited in silence as Gladdie returned to her numbers. Spruce finished his call and stepped back in. "Sorry about that."

"She wants to go out," Gladdie said, not missing a beat on the calculator.

He laughed. Kes did not. "There aren't any spare

boats around," he said, now serious. "This is a working dock, ma'am."

"Detective," she corrected him. "And you're Spruce?" She wasn't sure she had heard correctly.

"That's what they call me. Like the tree."

She wondered if it was his name or a nickname. It suited him. "This is a police investigation. A missing girl was last seen on the wharf yesterday morning. I need to see the shore from the water. If she fell in—"

"If she fell in, she could be a hundred miles down the coast," Gladdie chimed in. "You gotta think of the drift, ebb, slack, and then you gotta add wind and the current's set. People think water stands still." She didn't have any patience for people who didn't know the sea.

"Gladdie." Spruce gave her a "calm down" look.

"I'm here to find a missing girl who could be somewhere out there," Kes appealed to Spruce. "Someone whose family is looking for her."

Spruce considered. Kes noted his weariness, this man with fisherman's hands, cooped up in an office. She wondered what had brought him inside.

"I can take you out tomorrow," he said.

"It's Dumping Day," Gladdie protested.

"I'll help you when I get back, Gladdie. The boys will understand."

Kes calculated the time. "Tomorrow will be thirty-six hours since the girl went missing. That's too long," she said.

"We gotta wait on the tide." Spruce settled into his chair. "It's almost the end of day. Get some dinner, have a good sleep, we'll head out in the morning. You don't want to go in the middle of the night."

"I think I do," Kes said. "What if she's alive out there?"

"Oh fer shit's sakes," Spruce muttered.

Kes didn't take it personally. She saw a tired man carrying a load of responsibility, accustomed to keeping an even keel. And she had arrived like a storm.

"Sorry, Detective, it's been a long day and now it's gonna be a longer night. When's our next one, Gladdie?"

Gladdie reached for a well-worn tidal chart. "One-fifteen, but you want to be there for the slack, twenty minutes earlier."

"Yes, thank you, I know that, Gladdie."

"For her benefit, not yours," she said. "The day you don't know these waters is the day we dry-dock you."

"She's a sea witch at heart," he quietly confided to Kes. It sounded like a compliment.

Kes was certain Gladdie had heard by the small smile she hid as she put her glasses back on.

"Okay, Detective. You pay my gas, time, and any damages. Be on the dock at 12:30 sharp. And wear something warm. I recommend getting some sleep before then. We'll have a window of about four and half hours out there." He picked up his phone. "Jeezus, twenty messages."

"I'll be there." Kes headed for door. "I have one more question."

"Shoot," Spruce said.

"For Gladdie."

Gladdie peered up at Kes over her glasses.

"If someone did fall in around the time you saw the girl, based on drift, ebb, flow, slack, wind, and the current's set...where do you think a body might land?"

Gladdie eyed Kes anew. "That's his domain," she said. "I just push the paper."

Kes looked to Spruce, who turned to the map on the wall. Under his breath, she could hear him reciting a series of times, speeds, and directions. He touched the point across the bay. "I'd be looking there."

"Then that's where I want to go," Kes said.

"Did you factor in temperature?" Gladdie asked.

Spruce gave her a look. It seemed like this was a game they often played. The deep respect between them was palpable. Spruce slid his finger over half a degree.

VII.

KES PULLED INTO THE ORCHARD WAY MOTEL PARKING LOT AND backed into a space near the office. It was a clean, family-run affair nestled in a grove of trees and had a large pond out front with ducks swimming in it. She opened the office door and a bell chimed above her. A young woman with a child perched on her hip came out of the back room. Kes could smell supper cooking and realized how hungry she was.

"Hi, I'm Detective Morris. You have a room booked for me?"

"I do. Number seventeen at the far end of the lot. I left your key in the door. Any luck finding that girl? Kinda creepy knowing she stayed in the same room the other night."

Kes was surprised this woman knew about the girl, but realized that news, especially bad news, travelled quickly in small communities. "How'd you hear about that?"

"Gladdie at the fish plant. She's my godmother. I'm Jillie. She said you'd be here in a few minutes."

"Do you know if there was anything left behind in that room?"

"Just the usual. Wine bottle, garbage, dirty linens, towels. Cleaned the room myself."

"Can you tell me anything about the girl? Your impression of her?"

"Never saw her. Her boyfriend paid and collected the key. They didn't have a reservation. He asked about a good place for dinner."

"Thanks." Kes was famished. "Where did you recommend they should eat?"

"On Main Street there's a wonderful Austrian place. A bit fancy but not that expensive. For something publike with good food there's the Wheelhouse."

"Great," said Kes, "and for coffee?"

"There's a German place just down from the pub for the best coffee and pastries in the morning. Doesn't open till ten though."

The woman shifted her toddler to her other hip. A little boy. He was almost asleep. His head was tucked into his mother's shoulder and his thumb was in his mouth.

Kes smiled. "How old?"

"Eighteen months. He never makes a fuss, this one." The woman beamed and kissed the top of his head.

Kes loved that age. "Mine fell asleep the same. Always wanted to be close."

"It's the heartbeat. I like to think that sound will be with him always."

Kes hoped so, because she was about to break her daughter's heart again. She had promised to pick her up after school tomorrow.

Someday, maybe Olivia would understand why a missing girl had to come first.

The room was simple, clean. A little hot. Two double beds. The view overlooked the parking lot and duck pond. Kes tossed her shoulder bag on a bed and opened the window. She walked the room in a grid pattern. She looked in drawers, flipped through the requisite Bible, checked the closet, under the bed, under the phone on the nightstand, behind the TV, and the bathroom for anything that might have been left behind. The trashcan was empty. There wasn't a speck of dirt on the floors or sills. If there had been any evidence here, the owner had polished it away.

Kes sat on the edge of the bed closest to the window and watched the ducks bob and preen. She made the call and hoped her ex wouldn't answer. But he did.

"Hi, it's me. I wanted to let you know I may not be able to pick Olivia up after school tomorrow." Kes focused on the ducks and let Henry's predicted anger spill over her. "I was called back early. A small case, not even really a case."

A tiff broke out; beating wings and pecking bills. "It's my job." The two ducks continued to rise out of the water, chests high, wings colliding. "I know." She let him vent, reminding herself not to cut him off. "There's still a chance I'll be back in time." She could hear his girlfriend in the background and Olivia's laughter.

One duck retreated, only a few feet, but it was enough. The other charged and the loser turned. "I have to do this," she said. "I'm hoping you can cover for me. I haven't missed anything in months. If I can make it, I will."

The ducks circled the small pond, a comical chase, until the victor was satisfied and they took to opposite sides to tend their ruffled feathers.

"Thank you and I'll let you know—"

He hung up on her.

She watched the pond, serene now. A lost feather floated on the surface and she felt the weight in her heart. Her eyes pricked.

Kes drove to the Wheelhouse for an early supper. The main street was a lovely tree-lined avenue that passed by an old French fort and botanical gardens, and veered slightly where it followed the tidal basin. The restaurant was situated in a converted warehouse overlooking the tidal flow beneath a power station's turbines. It announced itself with a bright pink neon sign.

She was surprised the tavern was so busy. The bar seats were taken and she had to wait. As soon as a table emptied, it was cleared, reset before the previous customers were out the door, and immediately filled. The staff never lost track of who was next in line. Most were addressed by name. A restaurant where locals came was usually a good sign. And presumably an outsider like Molly would have stuck out. It was possible, if she and Lucas had come here the other night, someone might remember them. It wasn't long before Kes was ushered to a small corner table in the back.

"Specials today are two-piece fish and chips or hot turkey sandwich," informed the server before blowing her bangs from her forehead. "Something to drink?"

"Are the fish and chips good?"

"That's what we're known for. Fresh, lightly breaded, and comes with awesome coleslaw."

"I'll have that and whatever's local on tap."

The woman nodded; no notepad, all memory. "I'm Marion. Holler if you need anything."

"I do have a question." Kes stopped her. "You happen to notice two young people here last night? Not local."

"Burger and fries and pan-fried haddock and salad. From the city. Sat at the bar. It was jackpot trivia night, full house, everyone else was regulars."

"How did they get along?"

The server shrugged. "Sweet, I'd say. She was all over him. Think he was going to have a lucky night. He paid. Tipped well for a kid. Seemed like he was trying to impress her." A bell rang in the kitchen. "I gotta get that."

The fish and chips were as described and Kes could have had seconds of the coleslaw. She checked her watch. She'd still have a couple hours to sleep, though she wasn't hopeful her mind and body would comply. She reviewed her notes as she waited for the bill and nursed the last sips of her beer. In the margins she wrote in rough tide times. Six hours apart. High, low. She looked at the words on the page. *Abduction?* No witnesses. *Willful disappearance?* Then why? *Accidental death?* Most likely. Fell in the water unnoticed.

Kes stared at the page until it become water in her mind. She stood at the edge of the dock. Drowning is a quiet event. That's what people get wrong. It's silent. She slipped into the water. Cold, much colder than expected. A cold that took away her breath. A camera strap around her neck. Near high tide, twenty feet of water in the harbour. The wharf right there...the ladder rungs...the men working on the boat right there...all she had to do was yell, but the pull from below, head tilted back, still believing she could get out, gulping for air, unable to make a sound, her head dipping under, a slow descent into salt water, clogging the back of her throat, filling her nose...

Kes's phone rang and she inhaled. The sounds of the tavern flooded back in. She fished her phone out of her bag. The room's light seemed watery. Kes grounded herself to the floor, to the table...her phone kept ringing. The table next to her glared their displeasure. She mouthed "sorry," switched the phone to silent, and checked the screen. *Bjorn*. Marion returned with her bill and Kes smiled her thanks.

"Bjorn, nice to hear you. I'm so sorry about tonight."

"Someone's been killed?"

"What?"

"You were called away on a case?"

He knew. She was caught. She had lied to an ethics professor. "How did you...?"

"Search engine, dear Kes. You told me you worked at the police station, not that you were their exalted lead detective."

"It's more of an omission than a lie." But that also tasted like a lie. Friggin' technology; there was nowhere to hide anymore unless you were guilty. She hated that she could be found so easily.

"A gentle deceit is still not the truth. Perhaps you shouldn't have said anything at all?"

"Probably so." So this was goodbye. Kes had wanted to tell him the truth. Wanted to for weeks. But to claim one side of her story meant she had to claim the rest. "I just wanted to wait and see how we went."

"You mean, give you time to decide if you were going to want to stick around?"

Her defences caged around her. What she liked about him was his ability to see what most missed in her, but that's also what made her wary. What was she supposed to tell him, a civilian? Her stories weren't first-, second-, or even third-date material. That she had told him she had a daughter should count for something. If it was over, she didn't need to be reprimanded.

"What about you checking me out on the internet? You could've just asked me. Is that not a shading of truth?"

"I'm really not sure about that, public domain and all. One big ethical grey area at the moment." He laughed. "So, a raincheck for when you get back to the city?"

He wasn't running. Kes wasn't sure how to respond. She'd been ready for a fight, the disappointment, the shaming, the guilt. "That would be nice," she said.

"You tell me what you can, when you're ready. I look forward to getting to know you, Detective Kes Morris."

When she hung up, Kes breathed out a tension she hadn't realized she was carrying. She hadn't wanted Bjorn to leave. She held that realization uncertainly. He hadn't judged her. Not yet anyway. There was plenty of time for that. But for now, they had more time and that didn't scare her. She was hopeful she might be home tomorrow, but immediately regretted that thought, because it would mean she had found Molly dead.

VIII.

Kes heard something. Muffled and low. She was walking down a hall. It was dark, but there was a soft, dim light coming from the room ahead. It seemed familiar, oranges and greens. Her feet were bare and she was young. And she was scared. The sound was louder the closer she got. It sounded like crying. Guttural and stifled, like a hand held over a mouth. There was an open bottle and her daddy's back was to her. His revolver was on the table and his badge beside it. *Dad*, she said and the word sounded far away.hidden He looked back at her and quickly covered what was on the table with a newspaper, but he kept crying.

She was making a sandwich, peanut butter and jam. Her dad was still crying and the newspaper was still on the table. She set the sandwich in front of him, because that was all she could think to do. He looked up and said, "I have to tell you something." But his lips didn't move. "Don't forget..."

Alarms went off. Smoke? Sirens? Something on fire? Closer now, police? Why were they here? She turned to the door, raised her hands in surrender. "I'm a detective," she hollered and the door burst open...

It was dark. Kes had forgotten to leave on a light. On the nightstand, an alarm clock screeched: 11:30. Morning. No, night. Where? Her phone alarm went off next. She reached for the radio clock to shut it off, but couldn't find the button. She swiped the darkness for the lamp and knocked over the motel phone. It clattered to the floor. She silenced the clock radio. Grabbed her cellphone and hit snooze. Remnants of the dream ghosted inside her. No matter how many times she dreamed it, she never reached the end. She was always twelve. It was always the night her mother left. She wasn't even sure if she remembered making a sandwich, but it's the story her father used to tell her. He said she'd saved him.

Kes wiped the sleep from her eyes. Her head was groggy. To her surprise, she had slept for five full hours. She sat up, fully clothed, and eyed the coffee machine. Crappy instant coffee and powdered milk mix. She picked up the phone from the floor and set it back on the table. That's when she saw a flash of white between the wall and nightstand. She edged the table out and retrieved a torn fragment. On it were handwritten numbers. A sequence with no breaks or hyphens. A phone number? Molly's or a previous guest's?

She dialled.

This number is not in service, droned the recording.

Her snooze alarm went off. She tucked the paper inside her notepad and looked to the cheap coffeemaker, paper cups, and powdered milk packs. She let the alarm ring another five minutes, until it no longer made her heart beat fast.

Kes pulled into a spot in front of the fish shacks. At night, lit overhead, the buildings seemed even richer in colour. Spruce was standing at the edge of the wharf talking on his phone. She grabbed her sweater, shoulder bag, and two paper cups. He hung up on her approach.

"Right on time," he said.

"I try to be." She handed him a coffee. "Motel. Best I could do." She took a sip. It was bitter and lukewarm.

"So long as it's caffeine." He took a swig. "I've had worse. Made it yourself?" He downed it and tossed the cup into a bin. "Thanks." She couldn't finish hers.

"You don't get seasick, do you?"

"Not as yet," she said.

"It's different at night. You don't have the horizon to balance you. You have to give yourself over to the sway and roll."

"Which one is yours?" She looked out over the crowd of boats laden with lobster traps. The wharf and boats were starkly lit with industrial lamps. Harsh light ringed by night.

Spruce pointed to an old fishing trawler about five feet beneath them. *The Gladdie May.* "'Bout ten more minutes till she'll be floating well enough for us to head out. Sure you want to do this?"

"I am." Kes pulled on her sweater. It didn't have the heft of his, which looked handmade.

"Yeah. Bert said you were a bit full-bore."

She wasn't sure if that was an insult or a compliment. "Bert?"

"The chief. My brother."

Kes searched for a family resemblance. It wasn't physical. Bert was rounded and sloped, whereas Spruce was solid and upright. Maybe the eyes.

"All right, Detective Morris, climb on down the ladder, face the wharf. I'll be right behind you."

The metal rungs were slimy, wet, and cold. As Kes stepped down she could see that the dock pylons and the underside of the wharf were teeming with life. She was amazed by the array of mussels, barnacles, periwinkles, and seaweeds that had attached themselves to the structure. All that life, right beneath their feet. A small crab scuttled out and Kes pulled her hand back quickly.

Once they were both onboard, Spruce pulled a long wooden pole from under the seat and stuck it in the mud over the side of the boat, checking the depth. "Five more minutes and we can start our voyage." He carefully tucked the pole back under the seat. He loosened the cat's cradle of lines around the boat, coiling them and tossing them up onto the wharf, until they were tethered by only one.

Kes watched how nimbly he moved around the vessel. "It's quite a process here," she said, "dealing with the tides."

"You get used to it. It's a reminder each and every day of who holds the power in these parts. And it sure ain't us." Spruce started the engine, kicking water around the stern.

"When Gladdie said she saw that powerboat, the tide would have been coming in, correct?"

"Yup, bit higher than now, but still goin' up."

"So, the current would be pulling that way?" Kes pointed in the direction of the narrows.

"Yup. And just after the tide's in it pulls the other direction." He switched on the green-and-red sidelights, the white stern light, and a row of bright floodlights on the cabin. Even illuminated, the water looked black and she could see trickles of slick oil on the surface.

Spruce nudged the throttle and tossed away the last line. Muddy brown water surged behind them. Kes glimpsed pieces of rusted metal, tangled nylon rope, and silver darts of fish beneath the surface. They slowly skirted the seawall. The cabin lights lit everything stark and flat.

"We'll head straight to Birch Cove then cross at The Five Sisters. Takes a bit longer, but you'll see more." He pushed the throttle forward and the bow lifted before settling, and they rounded the seawall into the basin. Suddenly, they were in a cold breeze, much cooler than ashore. The lights shone easily three hundred yards ahead, cutting a sharp swath into the night. She could see nothing beyond the funnel of light. The engine purred quietly, surprising for such an old boat.

Behind them, Spectacle Harbour looked like a perfect miniature. Spruce flipped off the floodlights and they plunged into blackness. Kes reached for the cabin to stay the sensation of falling.

"Give it a few moments," Spruce said beside her. "Your eyes will get used to it."

She tried to settle into the dark and closed her eyes to fight a wave of nausea. She couldn't find the rhythm and stumbled into the gunwale.

"Anchor yourself to the deck," Spruce said softly.

Kes widened her stance and soon she was moving with the gentle roll. She opened her eyes and the pitch black softened to grey and soon she could differentiate the water, then the crests, and finally the glisten of moonlight shimmering all around them. Where the breeze hit the water, the light broke into ripples that looked like gems. It felt wonderful to be breathing in the cool, fresh air.

Kes settled into the rise and fall of the boat. It nosed south, seemingly away from the point. "Aren't we heading over there?"

"We ride it in instead of fighting our way against the current." Spruce's eyes were fixed ahead. "It's almost time." He slowed.

"For what?" The boat tugged and pulled in the growing, unsettled chop. The water seemed to be flowing in two directions.

"The slack," he said and cut the engine. It was dead quiet. They were in the middle of the bay and the water stilled. Flat calm. "This is the only time she stops moving," Spruce said quietly. "This is my favourite time. The sweet spot." The boat was stalled in the stasis of the incoming and outgoing tide.

They listened in silence. Around them, seaweed floating on the surface was motionless. Over there, a driftwood log was suspended. There wasn't a ripple on the water. Kes could see the moon in its reflection and stars if she looked deep enough. She turned to take in the breath of calm. Off the portside, there was something else held by the water. She tried to sort out its shape. A seal? No, bigger. A porpoise? The hump of a whale? It couldn't be. She didn't sense anything watching her.

"Spruce? What's that?"

"Where?"

"Off the stern."

He looked over his shoulder. "Flotsam? Tons of debris gets washed into this bay. Maybe a jacket blown overboard? All the junk people toss. Everything shows itself in the stay, before getting pulled under again."

She could see what looked like arms now. It was a jacket, limp and splayed, but sitting high in the water. "Can we get closer?"

Spruce turned on the engine and reversed slowly. The jacket swayed in the churn of the propeller. Molly hadn't been wearing a jacket.

"There's a gaff hook under the seat. Haul it in. Get another piece of trash out of the bay."

Kes retrieved the hook and Spruce expertly swung the stern around and cut the engine. The boat drifted towards the coat. The port light painted the water red. Kes reached over the gunwale and snagged the fabric. It was heavy. She tugged and lost hold.

"We don't have much time," Spruce warned, "she's about to wake."

Kes looked out and could see the water starting to roil beyond their diminishing calm. She reached again and the hook splashed heavily, missing its target.

Spruce joined her, taking the gaff hook. "I got it." He swung it wide, catching a sleeve, and pulled it towards them. "It's balled up with kelp or something." The sleeve slipped away and he raked across the fabric, hitching the middle. It was only a few feet away. The coat rolled and a man's head emerged from under the water.

"Jesus Christ!" Spruce jerked back. He dropped the hook and it was dragged overboard. "What the hell?"

The body shifted clockwise and the boat counter-clockwise. The water churned around them. "Tide's turning, we gotta move." He raced back for the wheel.

The body was on the starboard side now. Kes followed it. "We can't lose him!" She hung over the gunwale and grabbed the collar. It dragged her towards the bow and she braced against the rail. She could feel the burn of wood under her arm.

"I gotta start her up!" Spruce hollered back.

The engine roared and Kes grabbed the rail to keep from toppling over. She could smell fuel. The water was moving in multiple directions. "I can't hold on!"

Spruce slammed the throttle into neutral and ran back. The boat was spinning. He reached down, grabbed hold. "One-two-three: heave!"

The body lurched to the top of the gunwale. Using all their weight as a fulcrum, they tipped it back. It thudded to the deck and the boat spun wildly, driven by the outgoing current. Spruce ran for the controls and revved the engine. He spun the wheel and the boat shuddered and listed portside.

Kes looked for shore. Spectacle Harbour was nothing but faint pinpoints of light, now off the bow, no longer behind them. The moon starboard...

Spruce jammed the throttle full. Kes was thrown back against the stern. Around them the water whirlpooled. She saw the driftwood log get sucked away and disappear. And in an instant the current changed, the sea flattened, the boat settled, and they were riding the tide. The village was behind them again. The moon ahead of them. And a corpse at Kes's feet.

IX.

Spruce was cursing, panicking. "I gotta call this in." He fumbled with the marine radio and dropped the handset. "Fuck." He turned to Kes. "We gotta go back."

"Spruce..." She focused on him. "I need a minute." She needed him calm. "It's going to be okay. Keep the boat steady, straight ahead. Can you do that?" He complied, relieved to have a simple direction. He turned his back from the horror and stared mutely ahead.

Kes knelt down. She felt the calm detachment and heightening of her senses. She could see the body clearly in the moonlight. Male, older. Fifties, sixties. Eyes open. His coat appeared to be wool or camel hair with leather trim that had suffered from the salt water. In his hands was a boat's steering wheel. Small, polished, inlaid. Mahogany? He was lashed to it with rope. A piece of the shaft was still attached to the wheel. The metal was bent and snapped. She rolled up the remnants of the shredded pant. The leg was flayed above the knee, the skin hanging loose to the ankle. She could see the bulge of the severed tendon coiled up in the groin area. There were raking, saw-like marks on the upper thigh and the shorn femur jutted out.

"Spruce? Could a propeller do this?"

He glanced back and immediately looked away. "I

don't friggin' know. Maybe a shark? Poor bugger. That's some brutal way to go." She could hear a quiver in his voice.

"Do you have something I can cover him with?"

"Tarp's under that seat."

Kes fumbled with her phone camera. Her hands were stiff and numb from the cold water. She took photos of the face, wheel, knots, and ravaged leg. She looked at the face again. Shaven, clean-cut. No ID in the pockets. She draped the tarp over the remains. The motor hummed. She stood and, for a moment, lost her bearing again. She breathed out and tried to find the deep ink of the horizon. The dark silhouette of the opposite coastline emerged from the night sky. Close. They had crossed the bay.

"Spruce, turn on your lights."

Blinding white light flashed and towering red cliffs shocked the darkness. And then they saw it.

Jammed against a rock spit was a mahogany speedboat lodged between two large boulders.

"Isn't that where you and Gladdie thought we might find something?"

"Damn," Spruce muttered as he nudged his boat closer to the shattered hull. He checked the bearings. "I didn't think we'd be right."

"What'll happen when the tide pulls out, Spruce? Will it still be there next high tide?"

"She's taking on water. The bow looks pretty smashed up by the way she's listing. She could pull free."

"Can you get me close enough to check it out, while there's still a boat?"

"No friggin' way!" He raised his voice. "I've got a corpse on my boat and a tide pulling out. I'm not getting grounded out here with that."

"I don't need a lot of time." Kes wasn't giving up. They were closer now, within fifty yards; Spruce was having to navigate into the current to keep them from overshooting the boat. "There's a sand beach just behind us. You could drop me off. Radio your brother. Have him meet you with the medical examiner and ask him to have an officer drive around to pick me up."

"That's an hour and a half drive! I can't leave you out here that long."

"It may be the only shot to retrieve any evidence. That's a probable crime scene now and I take full responsibility."

He looked to the mounded tarp on the deck. "Damn rights you do."

"I'll be okay," she reassured him. "I have my phone. I'll be here waiting."

"That'll be useless up here. And there's bears. You got a gun?"

She hadn't considered bears. "Yes," she lied. It was in the lockbox in the wheel well of her trunk.

"Sure hope you know what you're doing." Spruce nosed the boat towards beach. "Take that pole under the seat to help your balance. And a flashlight. You gotta watch the current. It can sweep you right off your feet."

Kes jammed the flashlight into her bag and grabbed the wooden pole, which was actually a hand-stripped hardwood sapling, straight and strong. It fit her hand perfectly. She could feel the indent and smoothness of the grip worn down by Spruce.

"The road runs close to the cliffs. Through those breaks there's deer paths to lead you up. That's where I'll send the car."

The little protected cove was clear and deep. Spruce reverse throttled to swing the stern around. The boat slowly drifted towards a large, flat rock. Kes stood up on the gunwale.

"Use the pole to check the depths." He nudged the throttle back. "I can't go any farther or I'll ground."

Kes drove the stick into the sand, only a foot's length protruding, and used it to pivot herself onto the flat-topped rock. Two more leaps from rock to rock and she was on land. Only one foot splashed in a shallow and the cold seared. If Molly was in the water she would be dead by now. "I'm good," she hollered back.

Spruce gunned the engine; he was already on the radio. The boat did a wide arc and headed towards Spectacle.

For a long time, Kes could hear the motor and when that died out, only the lap of waves. She stood in the cold of the night and felt the chill. She braced herself for what she might find on the abandoned boat. This was her job. She let the emotion drain, locked up her fear, and headed towards the wreck.

Kes navigated the tumble of rocks, her hand steadied against the sheared rockface looming above her, using the pole for balance. She easily traversed the narrow strip of beach marked with animal prints. She could smell evergreen and taste salt. Now that she was alone, the night seemed even brighter, and she followed her own moon shadow.

Sounds heightened and Kes could hear small twigs rustling and the lap of water. She had to hug the rock split to ease herself around to the battered boat. It was wedged in tight. Cracked just above the keel, water had breached the hull.

Kes looked across the bay and could just discern Spruce's stern light. She turned on the flashlight and bugs swarmed the beam. She looked up the cliff to the overhang, tangled with exposed roots. It looked like it could crumble any moment. She squeezed between the rock and hull and found she could step onto the gunwale, splayed on its side.

It was a custom-crafted boat with inset brass fittings, stainless steel flanges where the bumpers would hang, and brass handrails around the exterior. It reminded her of the sleek wooden water taxis in Venice, a trip she and Henry had taken when they found out they were pregnant. She remembered thinking that life had finally turned a corner for her.

She propped the pole against one of the white vinyl seats and shone her light across the helm. The steering shaft was snapped where the wheel should have been. The wheel that was now tied to the victim. She moved to the console and peered through the low windshield with its two wipers and looked down at the bent column. It didn't appear to have been sawed through or tampered with. This was definitely the victim's boat, or at least the boat he had been driving.

She scrolled through the photos on her phone until she came to the man's face. A broad face, tanned, longish sandy-brown hair. Trying to look younger than he was, she supposed. She took several photos of the damage and noted she didn't have a cell signal.

She tucked the phone away and worked her way across the askew deck to the cabin. She had to stoop to climb down the short, off-kilter stepladder. Below deck was surprisingly roomy. The wood gleamed. She could faintly smell varnish. It was obvious the boat was well taken care of. In some ways it made her think of her dad's Jag. She looked to the bed tucked up in the forward berth. It was sharply made, unused. The hull's splintered wood sheared at the crisp sheets and dark water leached up the mattress. She stepped through the few inches of water seeping onto the floor and checked two small cupboards. Rain gear and tools. No other bodies below deck. No sign of a struggle. No blood.

She returned to the upper deck and looked to stern. The boat appeared intact. The floorboards shone. She went to the broken steering column and stood before it. The key was still in the ignition. No lights switched on. Could this have happened in the daytime? The throttle was jammed on high. Full speed. Set to plow directly into the cliffs? She wondered how fast this boat could travel. Gladdie had described the boat as *Money—loud*. Standing at the helm, Kes shut off her flashlight and imagined the drone of the engine, revved high. Slicing through the water.

His hands lashed to the ship wheel and column, around his wrists, unable to steer. Locked on a collision course. The cliffs racing towards him. Using all his strength to break the wheel free. Falling back when it let go. Still lashed. Did he choose to take his chances with the sea's mercy over ramming into a wall of rock? Kes was standing with her hands clenched, like she was holding the wheel. *How close before you jumped?* And the shocking cold. *How long did you tread water, the ship wheel hugged to your chest? Not long*, Kes thought. *Not long.*

And who did this to you?

The night filled with coyote howls and Kes turned to the sound. She couldn't discern the direction of their yelps. She cocked her ear. Above her. Not close. She looked across the bay. Spruce would be back in Spectacle by now and a squad car on its way to her. Chief Hawthorne would be waiting at the wharf. The medical examiner coming from where?

The coyotes were wailing. *A fight? A warning? Or bringing down prey?* Kes picked up the stick, turned the flashlight back on, and stepped off the stern. Already she could see a few more inches of fresh wet sand. High tide had crested. If Molly had been aboard, could she have survived the impact? Or was she, too, floating out there somewhere in the water?

Kes looked back at the broken boat and shone her light on the stern. Painted in gold leaf was the name *No Nonsense*.

Using the pole as a walking stick, Kes made her way up a gentle slope and an overgrown path. The beach grass gave way to meadow and rocks gave way to a forest of scraggly spruce, extinguishing the moon. Everything beyond the narrow flashlight beam was pitch black. She kept her eyes trained on the ground for a suspect or another victim's footprints, or both. *Molly's?* But all she saw were quad bike tracks. Maybe the locals came down to fish or hunt?

The woods opened on an untended field and the sky filled with stars. Kes shut off her light and stood there, looking up at its vast beauty. Something skittered nearby. *A mouse?* She headed up the sloping hill, following rock walls overgrown with moss and wild grasses. Cresting the hill, an abandoned farmhouse sat next to a secondary highway. Not far down the road, she could see the lights of a small community nestled in another cove. In the other direction, only darkness.

The house's white paint was peeling. The roof shingles were buckled and loose. Still, this had been a pretty structure once. Kes stepped carefully onto the rotten stoop. The door was locked. She peered inside a fly-specked window. She was surprised to see a kitchen table, chair, and vintage wood cooking stove and dishes next to a washing tub. A coat hung on a hook. It looked as though the person had just stepped away, but the calendar on the wall was dated twenty years past. Odd that the place hadn't been vandalized.

She checked the time. It would be at least an hour before her ride arrived. She sat on the stoop, shut off the flashlight, and immediately felt the weariness of a late night.

The house was perfectly perched on the cliff to overlook the bay. It must be an incredible view in daylight. The sound was different up here. She could hear scuttling through the tall grass. Close by, an owl hooted. And the coyotes were still howling. She thought about bears and made sure the stick was at hand. Far off, across the bay, Kes could see the twinkle of Spectacle Harbour.

She wondered what it would be like to live here. Her and Olivia. When she was in rehab, she had thought about leaving the force. Couldn't face her shame and the damage to her reputation. A reputation she had built on her ability to not break no matter the cost. She had tempered herself to not feel; to sacrifice herself for the greater good; that her job was bigger than her life.

Wasn't that what her father had taught her? But she had sacrificed her daughter, too. Like he had.

She learned that she could break in tiny white pills. Her dad broke in a bottle of scotch. Maybe she could move here. Start again. Leave the grime and horror behind. She and Olivia could disappear from the world and watch the sun rise and fall. Untouched by evil. Because there was evil in the world. She had seen it. Maybe, she could fall in love again. She and Olivia and someone like Bjorn. A decent man. Maybe they could be a family and she could learn to bake bread in the old oven and plant a garden over there. Maybe that life wouldn't be so bad.

Kes looked to the water, black and calm, and wondered how many bodies it had claimed. How many bones were at the bottom. When she was trying to pull the body out, she could feel the ice-cold skin. She could look in the eyes of the dead man and feel nothing. She could hoist up the victim's pant leg and brush her hand against the jagged thigh bone. She had looked to Spruce and seen him collapsing and couldn't understand his response, because all she had felt was the hunger of a new hunt. It was the first time she had felt alive since her world fell apart.

She had a missing girl and a dead man. Connected or coincidence? Her father used to say he didn't believe in coincidences. *Once you feel that knowing, that itch inside you,* he'd say, *it might be a wide circle, but it always loops back to the starting point.*

A coyote yowled closer. Kes howled back, and the night silenced.

X.

THE SQUAD CAR WAS WARM AND THE OFFICER YOUNG. KES WAS surprised to see a number of homes along the rugged shore under construction and renovation. There were signs for a gourmet restaurant coming. Change was underway, even on this remote point. The treeline grew denser and then there was nothing for miles and miles. She was lulled by the familiar cradle of a police car moving through the night and rested her head against the window.

How many times had she fallen asleep as a child in the hard back seat, watching the back of her father's head through the protective shield? Whenever she had a nightmare, he would take her for a drive. He always said she'd fall asleep before he made the first turn at the end of the road, but he'd keep driving long after. Sometimes, she woke up back in their driveway with her dad snoring and she'd stay quiet until he stirred.

The tires hummed and the white line on the shoulder streamed by and Kes dozed off. Dreamless.

It was almost 5:00 A.M. when they arrived back in Spectacle Harbour. Kes could see the deep twilight blueing on the horizon. The boats were sitting a good ten feet lower in the bay. There was a truck, car, and police vehicle at the head of the wharf and the medical examiner's van was just pulling out. An older man was talking to Chief Hawthorn.

"I'll get out here," Kes said to the officer. "Thanks for the drive." She grabbed the muddy pole wedged alongside her leg and threaded between the back divider. The young officer hadn't been keen when she'd insisted on bringing it along. He kept his car immaculate, like his uniform. She suspected he usually had plenty of time on his shifts to maintain them.

Chief Hawthorn looked up as she approached. "This is Dr. George MacDonald, attending physician from the medical examiner's office. He made the trip in from the city. This is Detective Kes Morris, the reason we're up at this time of night."

Kes took in the older man, a new transfer. His hair was unruly and fell shaggily below his ears. There was a fresh shaving nick on his left cheek. *Rumpled* was the word that came to mind.

"I thought I might see Connie here," Kes said.

"She's working reduced hours; seniority, you know. Practising for retirement. I hear she's bought a trailer up the coast and has taken up line jigging." MacDonald seemed to have a perpetual squint. "But really at her age, she needs more sleep. That's what I tell her anyway." His eyes were smiling. "I understand you found the body?"

"Well, more like it found us. We fished him out."

"Usually what's fished from these waters is more appetizing," MacDonald quipped. Kes appreciated someone who could smile in the darkest moments.

"Can you tell me anything yet?" she asked.

"On first look, I'm not sure whether he drowned or was dead upon entering the water." He looked to the pavement as though the body was still there and recited his findings. She stared at the same spot. She could see it too. "No sign of froth in his mouth or upper airways. Tongue not protruding. He hadn't been in the water long by the look of the skin. The palms, soles, and fingertips wrinkled and sodden, but not sloughing. Not waxy. No decomposition. Sea lice hadn't been feeding on him. Birds hadn't gotten to him yet either. There's serious bruising where he was lashed. Rope burns to the bone on both wrists. He fought hard to free himself. Any forensic evidence is probably washed away, but we'll see."

"Maybe the boat will tell us more. Is there a team with it?" she asked the chief.

"It's been organized." Hawthorn's answer was short and irritated.

"Whose jurisdiction is it? Are they there now?"

"I said, it's been taken care of." *Not in front of the examiner* was the subtext.

MacDonald took the cue. He gathered up his kit. "I'll know more once I get back. I expect you'll want answers as soon as possible. You all do. I'll handle this one personally."

Kes took in the doctor's deeply lined features and noticed another nick under his ear. There was nothing contrived about him. Even his shoes were aged and comfortable.

"Who should I ask for?"

"Try 'The Coroner.' It's not a great password, but it should do the trick. You haven't been to the new office yet, Detective. A lot has changed." He crammed himself into a small, practical car.

As soon as he pulled away, Chief Hawthorn couldn't hold his temper any longer. "What the hell were you thinking?"

Kes felt her blood stirring. "Sir?"

"Why the hell did you bring the body here? You found it on the other side. You should have sent him to St. Joseph. We got enough going on around here without having to deal with a body from outside our jurisdiction! Now my team's split on that side of the bay having to negotiate with the RCMP over there and the coast guard and the boat wreck. It's a friggin' bureaucratic nightmare."

"With all due respect, sir, jurisdiction isn't my concern. I'm here to solve a case. I set out with your brother. He was the fastest way—"

"He's a *civilian*! Did you even take a moment to think what that might do to him? Seeing that?"

Kes didn't have an answer. She hadn't considered the potential emotional impact on Spruce at all. He seemed so weathered and experienced, she had made a presumption and treated him like a cop. She had forgotten that once ordinary people look at death they can't look away, and she deeply regretted that.

"I'm sorry. It wasn't what I expected to find." Even to her, it didn't sound like an apology.

"What *were* you expecting? Molly floating out there?" Hawthorn's cheeks and neck had reddened and she wondered about his blood pressure. "How would that have been any better?"

He was right. She didn't like that he could read her so well. She tried to redirect him to the case. "I think Molly and this murder are connected, sir."

"There's absolutely no indication of that. I knew you were hotheaded, heard you didn't respect rules and protocols. Your reputation precedes you, Detective."

Kes let him vent. Stood cool in his heat, assessing her adversary. "I was looking for a missing girl, following standard procedures. Something you should have done."

"We know how to do our jobs, Detective," he growled. "Just because you and your higher-ups made this a special case doesn't mean we'll be ignoring the rules. The girl hadn't even been missing twenty-four hours, no evidence of foul play, no probable cause...yet you expected us to blindly follow you! This is my precinct, and it doesn't work that way here."

Kes realized her body had taken an offensive position. Her legs were apart and her feet rooted to the ground. She was the perfect distance for a round kick or a swing of the stick. Her anger prickled just beneath her skin. She was tired of explaining herself, tired of shoddy work and excuses. But mostly, she was angry with herself for putting a civilian at risk.

"Sir." She breathed in. "We have a missing girl, a dead man, a wrecked boat, and that boat last seen at this wharf...I'm just following the case."

"You brought my brother into this, Detective." Kes could see his pain and worry. "He has nothing to do with this world."

"I apologize. I'm truly sorry. I am." And she was. "But we're here now."

"Yes, we are." They stood in the moment of silence. The ting of boat lines and the lap of water dissipated their anger.

"Let's start again," the chief sighed. "I'll let you know what we find out about the boat."

"I'll head back and keep you informed about the medical examiner's findings," Kes said. "And I'll start talking to Molly's family and acquaintances."

Hawthorn nodded and got in his truck. He looked tired and sad.

"I am sorry about Spruce, sir."

"Why don't you tell him that yourself." Hawthorn started up his truck and pulled away.

Kes found the *Gladdie May* tethered at the end of the wharf. She had to climb down a long way to reach the deck, made more awkward carrying the wooden pole. She gently laid it on the seat.

"Thanks for bringing it back," Spruce said.

Kes looked to the wheelhouse. Spruce was seated at the bow deck with his back to the gunwale. She was surprised to find him still there.

"It's hard finding a good stick that fits your hand," she said.

Spruce's hands were clasped around his knees, reminding her of a small boy, hiding. He was staring at the spot where the body had lain. The tarp was a rumpled mess at the stern.

"What happens next?" He didn't look her in the eye.

"We find out who he is."

"I sprayed the deck down, but I don't know if I got it all." He glanced to the tarp. "I don't know what to do with that. Don't want it anymore."

"I can take it with me," Kes said.

Spruce looked up at her and his eyes had that sunken stare of someone who had seen too much. "I could never understand why Bert would want a job like that. Seeing the worst of everything. But he wanted to take care of this place where we grew up. Keep it safe."

"I'm sorry you had to see that," Kes said. "I'm sorry I put you in that position. You have to know you did a good thing, Spruce. We brought someone home. The body can tell us what happened."

"It doesn't bother you?" He wanted the truth.

It would be so easy to lie. Tell him it's her job. Explain how she's been trained to separate herself from the work. How she tries to follow her dad's lessons and finds outlets like running and tae kwon do to harness her emotions. Or she could tell him about the insomnia, the nightmares, the pills...and the parts of herself that are woven inextricably with the depravity she's witnessed. She could tell him about Olivia.

"I have to do my job." As if that explained it. She handed him her card. "If you need to talk, call me anytime. I find it helps to remember the good in your life, whatever or whoever that is." She again thought of Olivia. "Do something you love, it can help."

"That's always been taking this boat out in the bay." He looked to the black waters. "Now, I don't know."

"The water's everything it was before," she said. "But this time it gave us what we needed to find. I'm thankful for that." She gathered up the tarp. She was tired and her calves ached from climbing over rocks, one sock was still damp, and she was cold. "Maybe it's time to get some sleep. That helps, too."

"I think I'll stay awhile," he said. "Until we touch bottom. It won't be long now. I'll be good tomorrow."

Kes headed up the ladder, wishing she could sit with him until the mud hugged the hull. She stuffed the tarp in the Jag's small trunk and reached in her pocket. She froze. She had been reaching for a pill. She felt the teeth of craving inside her chest.

No, she thought. *No*.

The wharf lights shut off and the morning was grey-blue.

XI.

Kes woke at first light in the small motel room. She had decided to take her own advice and have a nap before driving back to the city. She pushed her hair from her face and it felt coarse and stiff and salted from the night. She could still taste the sea on her lips. Outside, ducks were quacking. It was time to get up. She'd be able to pick up Olivia after all. She lingered in the warmth of the thin sheets and rough bedcover and thought of Bjorn beside her. She pushed the image away and checked her phone. She had texted Captain Francis about what she had found, but hadn't heard back yet. Day shift would just be coming in.

Kes lay there a moment recalling the night before, but Molly kept creeping in. She left the unidentified body and focused on the missing girl standing at the wharf, the pleasure craft slowing, and her stepping on. It would have been prearranged. How did they know each other? Why set up a meet like that? Why use Lucas to get here? If it was arranged, then Molly went willingly. Was she another victim? Or did she overpower the man? How could she physically do that? Why? And where was she now?

Kes brushed the slate of her mind clean and fit the pieces together from another angle. Assume the boat victim and missing person weren't connected. Molly didn't get on the boat. Then, in all likelihood, she had fallen into the water. Both scenarios went nowhere, and neither felt right. Kes knew the fine line between wasting precious time and following a hunch. But if you didn't chase the phantoms and later found out they were real, you wouldn't forgive yourself. However, if you kept chasing them in the wrong direction, making up your own phantoms, the truth would escape your grasp.

Her phone pinged and then started ringing. Captain Francis had gotten her message.

On the way out of town, Kes stopped at the German bakery. A little bell tinkled as she opened the door. The shop smelled divine. The walls were lined with shelves displaying freshly baked breads and the glass counter held desserts she wasn't familiar with. A woman, her apron dusted in flour, came out from the back carrying a tray of pastries.

"Good Morning," Kes said. "Are you open?"

"Ja, ja. Welcome." The woman had an ease and a smile that made her feel like an old friend.

"I love your shop." It made Kes feel like it was the start of a good day.

"Danke." The woman slid the tray into the glass counter.

"What are those?"

"Gooseberry butter strudel tarts."

"They look wonderful. May I have one to go and a latte?"

"Of course."

The woman reached for a dainty little box for the tart.

"I'll just take it," Kes said.

"Good things should be presented," the woman said and Kes acquiesced. She looked around the room as the coffee grinder churned. There were family photographs and stencilled flowers on the walls. She looked up at the hewn timber rafters.

"Hier bitte schön." The woman set the box tied with a string and slid the latte towards her. The froth held a rising wave that encircled the cup and crested into a small heart falling back into the swirl.

"Oh, it's beautiful." It truly was.

"To carry you through the day," the woman said, like she knew exactly what Kes needed.

The drive back consisted of a series of shitty calls. A long discussion with Captain Francis about whether or not the body and boat were in separate jurisdictions, which she left to him to sort out. The next with Henry. She could pick Olivia up after school now, but he had already booked off work early. She had to listen to a lecture about how the world didn't revolve around her schedule before he finally agreed to let her have tomorrow morning's school drop-off, which wasn't the same. It would cut her time with Olivia down to an hour.

Kes tried to salvage the day and called Bjorn to tell him she'd be in town tonight if he was available for dinner, but only got his voice mail.

Then Chief Hawthorn called to update her about the boat. Kes pulled over to jot down notes. The same day the girl went missing, locals on the other side of the bay heard a crash in the evening. Second high tide was around 7:00 p.m. So Hawthorn guessed the boat hit shore somewhere between 5:00 and 8:00 p.m. Witnesses to the sound agreed it occurred before dark. Kids on their quads found the boat the next morning, which explained the tracks. Why they hadn't called it in, she could only guess.

But then Hawthorn shared the bad news. The boat was stripped sometime between when Kes was there and this morning, before the forensic teams could secure it. There were no useable fingerprints. Not much left of value on the boat. The salvagers probably came in not long after she left.

She couldn't believe it. Their only possible evidence had been compromised and carted off? "Kids went out and stripped a boat?" She wasn't buying it.

"It likely wasn't kids," Hawthorn said. "There's a lot of value in a boat. The mahogany alone is worth a fortune. The brass, electronics…and a fast boat like that, maybe they hoped there'd be drugs. If the captain's not aboard, it's fair game. Law of the sea."

"Anyone can just salvage whatever they find? Even if it's a crime scene?" Kes circled *Law of the Sea* on her notepad.

"Well, they wouldn't have known that. There's a lot of insurance wrecks up this way. Boating is an expensive hobby. Some try to recoup their losses and report their boats stolen, or slipped their mooring, or hauled out in a storm…others just sink them out of spite, nasty divorces and the like, and try to cash out."

Kes slapped her notepad shut. What was there to say to incompetence?

Hawthorn filled in the silence. "We have divers coming in later to search off the wharf."

About time, Kes thought. "Good," she said and hung up.

In her rear-view, Kes saw a transport truck approaching. She braced herself as it swept past. A load of timber, impossibly stacked, swayed the Jag in its draft. She looked to the forest and wondered how much was clear-cut just beyond view. Even up here, nothing was left untouched. She sipped the last of her cold latte and ran her fingers inside the cardboard box to lick the last delicious crumbs. The woman at the store had been right. It was a delight to open the box and the pastry had been a tonic for all the day's bad news.

Start the day again, she told herself and slipped the car into first gear. Her phone rang shrilly as she pulled onto the road. She juggled the phone with sticky fingers.

"Morris."

"Detective Morris?"

"Yes." The voice was young. Male.

"It's Lucas Knox, Mo—"

Her phone cut out. "Lucas? Wait, I can't hear you. I'm going over a hill, hang on..." She sped up and crested. "Lucas?"

"Molly just showed up. She's here! At school! What the fu—"

Her connection dropped.

Kes parked in a visitor's spot and headed to the university's administration building. A few students were sitting on the steps. She asked the man at the front desk where Molly Kinder's room was located.

"We can't give out that information."

She pulled out her badge. "Detective Morris. I need to ask Ms. Kinder a few questions."

"Do you need a warrant for that? I can get the registrar..."

This was going to take forever. "Where's the statue of the horse?"

"What?"

"The horse, big statue."

"South quad."

Kes didn't wait for more. She found the building easily. Stone, brick, and ivy. Stately and intimidating. Sitting on a bench, under a bronze statue of a rearing horse, was a young woman casually reading a book. Molly. She was certain of it.

"Molly Kinder?"

The girl looked up, then returned to her book.

"I have a midterm in twenty minutes." Kes heard it as "Piss off."

Kes gave her disrespect the benefit of the doubt. "I'm Detective Kes Morris. I've been looking for you."

Molly rolled her eyes and placed her book in her lap. "Why?" She wasn't intimidated.

"I went to Spectacle Harbour. You were listed as a missing person."

"I wasn't *missing*." She snapped the book closed. "Fucking Lucas."

"How did you get back?"

Molly's gaze shifted. Kes glanced over her shoulder to a group of young men in football jerseys coming around the corner. Loud and boisterous.

"I don't think that's any of your business." Kes was taken aback by the girl's brashness. "As you can see, I'm alive and well." She gathered up her books. "If you'll excuse me, I'm going to be late for my midterm."

Molly headed across the quad. She walked with confidence. There was nothing Kes could pinpoint as sexy in her demeanour, and yet she was turning heads. Expensive sweater, designer jeans, leather boots...the illusion of a regular joe, but her walk was noble.

"Molly," Kes called after her.

The girl looked back at her.

"What about Lucas? You just dumped him?"

Molly shrugged and smiled, the same false smile as in the photograph, and carried on her way.

XII.

Lucy insisted on calling the captain to notify him of Kes's arrival back in town, even though Kes could see him through the glass wall.

"That's okay," Kes said. "He's expecting me." She headed in.

Captain Francis was on the phone with his back to her. She heard him say "She's here now" and then he wheeled around and put the phone down. "I don't have much time. I have an interview in less than an hour."

"You sent me on a wild goose chase."

"I sent you on a case to ease you back in, Detective," he said, reminding her of her rank and his, respectively. "And you completed the assignment. You found Molly Kinder." He had the audacity to smile. "Welcome back."

"I didn't find her, sir. She *showed up*." Kes felt like a pawn in a game she didn't understand.

"I hear you went to her school?" He didn't offer her a seat.

"Yes, to confirm it was her."

"Apparently it was quite distressing to her, finding out the police had been looking for her, and that she had caused so much concern and wasted so many resources. She was very apologetic." The captain's manicured hands were clasped on top of his desk. Not a fingerprint smudged the glass.

"That's not the young woman I met," she said.

"Perhaps that's attributable to how you approached her."

Kes held her anger and met the captain's gaze. It felt like she was being reprimanded for doing him a favour off the books, one he had requested personally.

Francis stood and reached for his jacket and cap. "I've called Chief Hawthorn to call off the search and thanked him for his efforts." His pant seams were perfectly creased and his shoes shone. She could detect a whiff of musky cologne. He retrieved a folder from his desk and flipped through it. "It seems I spend most of my time these days talking to the media."

She could hear disappointment and resignation in his voice. She wondered what he had been like as a young officer. Ambitious. He looked up at Kes. "That's all, Detective."

"Captain, investigating homicides is actually my job. We still have a body and a wrecked boat, and I believe they're connected to Molly."

He shut the file folder. "Why would you think that?"

Kes had nothing but a gut feeling. "A woman who works at the fish plant saw Molly, or a girl fitting her description. Same pier, same time, the same boat that we later found on the rocks. Molly disappears and a corpse shows up. I don't trust Molly Kinder and I don't believe her story."

"Right. Well, it's not our jurisdiction." He checked the full-length mirror, tucked in the corner of his shirt, and placed his cap on his head. "I'll put Roberts on the case for follow-up with Chief Hawthorn, but I trust they'll request assistance if they need it."

"I was the detective on scene. I found the body. I was on the boat. I want this case, sir. It's my case."

The captain's back straightened and Kes saw a shift in his eyes. He had put on his mask for the public. "You're not the only detective on this force, Kes. It's not a one-person show. You have to trust your colleagues will get the work done."

Kes had a mouthful of retorts, but she bit her tongue. She swallowed the thin, metallic taste of salt and iron.

"You know the way out," he said as he headed for the door.

Kes ran down the six flights of stairs two at a time. She stormed to her car and slammed the door shut, and immediately regretted taking her frustration out on the Jag. She wanted to squeal out of the parking lot in a burn of rubber. Instead she grasped the stick shift and gloved the well-worn leather. Why would the Captain want her off this case? What didn't he want her to find?

She counted the street lights, the white cars in the parking lot, and was a quarter of the way through counting the chain links in the fence when she made herself stop. She missed how the pills used to edit out all the extraneous details. Smoothing everything like beach glass.

She focused on the sworl of the Jag's wood grain dash, slipped back to the bay, and pulled the body from the water. She walked across the broken boat's deck, retrieving every detail, looking for what she had missed. There was nothing to connect Molly with the victim. And yet...she knew there was something. She let herself drift back. She needed help. Which could get her in a shitload of trouble. She pulled out her phone and made the call anyway.

"Kes Morris! Is that really you?"

"I always forget the name comes up."

"I can fix that for you." He laughed. Of course he could.

"How are things, Chester? How's everyone doing over there?" She made herself go through the necessary small talk.

"Well, pretty good. You know Captain Puck retired a few months ago. He won the golf tournament this summer, brought the trophy around for us to see. That makes me and Harrison the veterans now." His voice sounded bright and engaged, no longer hesitant and unsure of himself. "How about you, Kes?"

"I've been good," she said. "I even took a vacation." It was hard to lie to him.

"Holy shit," he said. "I didn't think you knew that word."

"Just barely. Listen, I'm calling on business. You still a tech wiz?"

"Hell yeah. I have all kinds of new toys."

"I have a request. You can say no."

His voice lowered. "So, this isn't an official request?"

"No, it's not. It's personal."

"What do you need?"

"I need info on a young woman named Molly Kinder, father's a senator. And also a boat called the *No Nonsense*. Registration, ownership, ports of call, etcetera. Whatever you can find."

"There was a horse called *No Nonsense* once, a jumper I think, or maybe dressage? Set an auction record." Kes was always amazed by the details in Chester's head. "Do I want to know anything more?" he asked.

"No."

"Okay." He laughed. "I'll get back to you. It was good hearing from you, Kes."

"You, too, Chester. I owe you one."

She hung up and looked out at the parking lot and returned a few waves from cops heading in and out of the precinct. She knew she was rubbing up against the line, but convinced herself she was still on the right side. Her phone dinged.

A text from Bjorn: *Trattoria@7*. She still had time.

Set in the midst of an industrial park, the new forensics lab was an impressive modern design of glass and steel, unlike anything she had seen. The architecture was rather beautiful in its line and proportion. It did not look like a place that housed death. There was an intercom next to the metal door. She pressed the buzzer and then looked up to the camera to show her badge. "Detective Morris here to see 'The Coroner'."

The door buzzed open and Kes was startled by the cathedral ceilings and glass walls forcing the eye upwards to the sky beyond. It felt like a European gallery. She couldn't conceive how this space had politically or financially come together.

She was told the autopsy was just wrapping up and she could proceed directly to the morgue where, again, she had to buzz for entrance. The room was glacial white and flooded with sunlight from the high windows. Steel tables and instruments gleamed. There were three people in the room. All were masked and gowned, only one was wearing a latex apron. She recognized Dr. MacDonald's eyes peering at her from behind his mask.

"Welcome to our new home, Detective."

"It's unbelievable," she said.

"Long way from the mouldy basements and concrete blocks we once knew. We do it all here now. Autopsy, pathology, storage. Protocols have changed as well. This is my team: our technician, Reagan; our float, Megan, she's our liaison between the lab, paperwork, answering phones; and Len, our photographer. Team, meet Detective Kes Morris." The masked faces nodded back.

"Thank you for letting me join you." She hadn't mentioned she was off the case. "Do you want me to suit up?"

"Your DNA is all over the corpse from the original recovery, no point now," he said.

"Twelve minutes," Megan announced. The photographer stepped forward and took several photos of the mangled leg.

"Apologies. We're on a tight schedule. We have five more bodies to touch today."

"May I approach?"

"Please." He stepped aside. Her John Doe was on the table. The torso was split open in a clean Y incision and the skin folded back. The ribs around the sternum had been cut. The body cavity was lined with blue absorbent towels. The organs had been removed and stored in carefully labelled bags. The boat's steering wheel and ropes were laid out on another table.

"Is there anything you can tell me about him?"

"You could wait for my report, but I know you're keen. Most of the good ones are." His eyes were smiling. "Male, late fifties, early sixties. Six foot. Two hundred fifty pounds. No obvious signs of head trauma or physical assault prior to being tied up. Perhaps something was used to convince him to cooperate."

"A weapon? A threat?" Kes pondered.

The doctor shrugged. "I leave that to you. I won't have tox reports for several days. No sign of injection or indication of overdose. However, I can confirm he didn't drown. No water in his lungs."

"So he was dead before he entered the water?"

"Not necessarily. I think he bled out from a severed femoral artery, before he could drown. These are teeth marks," he said, pointing to the damaged limb. "Serrated. Almost sawed off. We retrieved one fragment. Don't know what type of shark yet. That was just bad luck. Our John Doe seemed to have a lot of that."

"So...you're saying he was alive when he went overboard?"

"I suspect so."

"How long was he in the water?"

"Hard to know. Not long likely, based on the water temperature and being lashed to that wheel. It would have been difficult for him to tread water. He could have floated on his back or done a dead man's float, if he wasn't panicking. Fifteen to thirty minutes max before hypothermia set in. It will take more time for tissue analysis and to calculate cellular breakdown."

Kes nodded. He was good. Concise, professional, detailed. "Do we have prints?"

"Unfortunately, the fingers are too sodden and distorted to be matched."

Kes looked to the evidence table. "Anything from the rope?"

"Constrictor knot, like a clove hitch but harsher. Near impossible to untie. The rope burns have cut through the wrists here." Dr. MacDonald gently held up one of the victim's hands. "He was pulling back with all his weight. Hyped on adrenalin. There is some light bruising across the back and chest, consistent with falling backwards, and the bruises on his chest match the wheel imprint. He fell back with force."

She looked to the corpse's tanned hands, no sign of a band mark. "He wasn't wearing a ring."

"No. John Doe's keeping his secrets close. We may get a hit with dental records. Reagan, do you mind?" The technician gently pried open the mouth to reveal back molars filled with gold fillings and one broken tooth repaired with a gold insert. "He was wealthy, it would seem."

"Nine minutes," Megan said.

"Okay, thank you, Megan. You may begin." Reagan folded the skin back in place and reached for the curved needle with waxed twine suspended from the ceiling. She began to loosely stitch the chest back together.

Dr. MacDonald stepped away and removed his gloves, disposing them in a biohazard bag, and then placed his apron into a sterile bin. Kes followed him to the door. The photographer was labelling photo cards and setting them in a storage box with an ID number. Megan had begun wiping down stations and placing tools into high-speed sanitizers. The whole team moved with a practised efficiency.

"Thank you," Kes said. "Please pass along my best to Connie."

"Will do. She thinks very highly of you."

Kes looked back to see the technician gently washing the body and Megan standing by to cover it with a white cloth. She was struck by the dignity and the quiet.

XIII.

Kes was wearing a floral print dress that made her feel somewhat awkward, but also a bit sexy. She typically avoided dresses, skirts, and blouses, preferring not to draw attention to herself. Rising through the ranks in a primarily male field, it had always been easier to just be perceived as "one of the boys." And she preferred jeans and T-shirts, something with pockets. But tonight, she felt good claiming this other part of herself.

The Trattoria was humming with happy people. Thomas, the owner, greeted her warmly. She had been coming here for years. She spotted Bjorn sitting at a table near the bar, which made her smile; which made her chastise herself for appearing too eager; which made her soften her smile. She joined him. He stood and kissed her on both cheeks.

"You look lovely, Kes."

He was wearing a beautiful cable-knit sweater. Everything about him was simultaneously casual and elegant. Completely at ease.

"Thank you." She tried to find a way to sit comfortably in her dress.

"Drink?"

"I wouldn't say no to a whisky sour."

Bjorn caught a server's eye and ordered a whisky sour for each of them.

"So…" Bjorn smiled playfully. "Nice to meet you, Detective Kes Morris."

They were jumping right in. "I'm really sorry about the other night," she began.

Bjorn stopped her. "No need to apologize. Marking papers is something I usually put off, but your absence gave me the time to do them."

"Are we okay?" she asked. "I should have told you who I was." She felt exposed in the thin cotton fabric.

"I believe that falls under normative ethics. A set of questions arising from how we think we ought to act. *Ought* is hard to define. I think you have an easy bye on this one, Detective."

He was parrying with her. "In my experience, *ought* isn't that ambiguous," she said. "My career is pursuing people who ought *not* to have done what they did." Bjorn laughed.

She didn't say what she ought not to have done, like coercing Spruce, knowing full well she'd expected to find a corpse, Molly's, not a John Doe.

"Where are you, Kes?"

He had seen her disappear. She wasn't accustomed to being seen. "Tonight, I'm here, where I ought to be." And it was where she wanted to be.

Their drinks arrived with dinner menus and a bowl of stuffed olives. They ordered the specials of the day: pasta vongole for her and gnocchi for him. They clinked glasses and fell into a pleasant conversation. Bjorn told her stories about his home in Denmark near Helsingør, his two sisters, two brothers, their small sheep farm, their little boat, fishing for herring, the sound of ice floes warming, and how he'd become interested in ethics when he found the work of Knud Løgstrup in his father's small library.

Kes loved his stories and the easy laughter between them. How he could share his most embarrassing childhood moments with the same joy as describing the first time he swam in the sea. He was completely open, his eyes always on her. When she spoke, he listened. Held space for her to tell him more. And she found herself wanting to tell him more.

Kes told him about being the only child of a police detective who loved fishing and whisky. About how he had taught her to shoot, and how he would hide objects around the house and in the yard for her to find. Sometimes he'd leave clues: a footprint, a scuff on the wall, an overturned chair. She even found herself telling Bjorn about when her mother left them, finding a note stuck to the fridge, and her father's month-long drinking binge afterwards. She felt her stories were safe with him. Something she had only ever felt with one man before, and she had married him. They didn't talk about her job. He didn't push her to reveal more. He seemed to know she would bolt and was prepared to wait for her to come to him.

They finished their meal, and after their plates and empty wine bottle had been cleared, Kes asked, "Is it more difficult to live a normal life knowing all you know from your studies? I mean, do you find yourself questioning *everything* you do or think?"

"Well, my area of expertise is meta-ethics or applied ethics. So, I believe that the best way to live is to question, no?"

She considered his statement. "Questioning can wear me down, but then I'm often dealing with the less savoury aspects of life or, more often, death. So, if I understand correctly, professor, your field of expertise is never assuming or taking the world at face value."

"I like the way you put that. It's unwise to simply accept what's around us. There are many narratives."

"But the answers, the actions, everything in my job is supposed to be black and white. Right or wrong." Kes was the feeling the wine, her hands were animated. "Sometimes they shift from one side to the other. More often it feels like infinite shades of grey. But then, how do you know where you are on that spectrum? How do you move inside of that?"

The conversation had veered from the abstract. She was asking for herself. She was a little drunk.

"Well now we're getting into my advanced course, dear Kes. Do you think we're ready for that?"

She laughed. "Maybe just dessert for now."

"And a glass of port?"

They placed their order and sat quietly looking at each other. Even silence felt comfortable. He slid his hand across the table and she slid hers, fingertips to fingertips. Her phone buzzed. She had promised herself she would ignore it tonight, but her body had stiffened and he had felt it.

"It's okay, answer it," he said.

She checked her phone. A text from Chester: *Found something. Best to talk. Call me.* She looked up to Bjorn.

"You have to go." It was a confirmation, not a question.

"I'm sorry." She laid some money on the table and got up to leave. "Thank you." She leaned in and kissed him, long and slow, and in that moment, she wanted to stay.

"Go," he said.

She didn't look back, and wondered what shade of grey she had just chosen.

Kes grabbed a glass of water, pulled out her notepad and pen, and dialled Chester.

"Hey, Kes, I should have bet you. The boat was named after that horse I mentioned." He didn't pause for small talk or hellos. She loved that about him. "Built in Italy and shipped here. Sole owner: Bertrand Silver. His wife owned the horse, a whole stable actually. They're known for the horse, sure, but they also run a big travel company: Slipaway Travel."

Kes scribbled in her notepad, wondering if any of this would lead back to Molly Kinder.

"Sending you a photo."

She tapped her phone and there he was. The victim. Standing beside a horse, champagne bottle in hand—younger, but definitely him. She circled the name.

"Mr. Silver was also known as a bit of a gambler/wheeler-dealer type and narrowly avoided arrest for a number of shady operations. Once, he was found with counterfeit hundred-dollar bills; another time, unregistered weapons; and in one instance, a Slipaway cruise boat was found with twenty kilos of cocaine onboard. Each time, Silver's lawyers got him off. Lack of evidence. Nothing leading to his direct involvement or knowledge. The stories on him run back years. Slippery guy, and very well connected."

Kes took a sip of her water. Maybe someone had put a hit on Silver, which would mean she was way off track. Maybe this wasn't a case she wanted to follow at all. She could hear her father's voice: *You don't get to choose your victims.*

"I couldn't find much on Molly Kinder. No social media presence, which is weird for someone her age. She's been kept out of the public eye. But her father, Senator Garreth Kinder, is another story. He was a judge on the city circuit, then head of the Police Review Board, now he's a senator and is still on the board. Kinder is known for being against early parole and believes in cutting social programs to increase military spending. Are you crossing paths with him? This is a guy you don't want to be on the wrong side of."

"Since when do I get on the wrong side of people?" She wrote *Senator Garreth Kinder* across from *Bertrand Silver*. And between the two names, she lightly jotted *Captain Francis?*

"I've just started researching the clan. Mrs. Peggy Kinder, nee Dawson. Graduated from technical college in applied arts. Married Garreth Kinder when he was a lawyer thirty-eight years ago, divorced six years ago. Loves golf and started a foundation that purchases exotic art to display in public buildings. Unfortunately, she's had medical issues. Disappeared from the public eye. Brain injury, maybe? I haven't got all the details yet. One daughter, Molly."

"This is great, Chester." She was finally on the scent of something. "You've given me a trail."

"You'll be getting my bill in the mail," he joked. "I'm just starting to look into the travel agency. Mrs. Kinder appears in a lot of promotional photos on the archived website. It appears she went on at least one trip every year, arranged by Slipaway, up until about six years ago, which coincides with the divorce. I'm working on the manifestos to piece together routes. How deep do you want me to go?"

"As far as it takes you. I have what might be a disconnected phone number, can you check it, too?"

"Sure, but I won't find much if it's a burner..."

Kes retrieved the paper fragment she had found at the motel and gave him the numbers. "Thanks, Chester. Really appreciate this."

"It's been fun. More fun than investigating who stole Mrs. Green's garden gnomes." He laughed, then she could hear him take a deep breath. "Is there anything else I should know, Kes?" He sounded more seasoned since she had worked with him last.

"Just make sure you're not leaving any tracks, and we haven't spoken."

"You be careful, too," he said.

She appreciated his concern. "You still have your camp?"

"I'm here now. Fire's on. Door's always open." He sounded good and relaxed, like he had come into his own. "I'll call when I have more."

Kes wrote *Molly* under her mother and father's names. No links yet. But the dead man had been identified. She would have to inform Captain Francis. How was she going to tell him she had information she wasn't supposed to be pursuing? She looked to her notepad and the victim's name centred on the page. What shade of grey was he?

It was getting late and Kes wasn't in the mood or headspace to work on it tonight. It had been a long day. Two long days, with only a few hours' sleep. Exhaustion seeped through her. She thought about surprising Bjorn.

Knocking on his door. Curling up with him. She craved human touch. But she had left him at the restaurant. She had made her choice. She felt a pang of loneliness. It was her own fault. Her obsessiveness was always to blame. She could have waited to call Chester tomorrow. Some choices were black and white, after all.

XIV.

Kes waited in the townhouse's front hall to take Olivia to school. It smelled of fresh paint. She recognized an old jacket of Henry's hanging on a hook amidst trendier, newer ones. She counted the shoes, his and hers and Olivia's, lined neatly on racks. She wasn't invited in. She apologized again for disrupting Henry's schedule, but he didn't seem to forgive her. She doubted he ever would. She had to accept that as a consequence of her past. She had told him she was too sick to call when she admitted herself, pneumonia. She took the shaming. For the first time, grateful that he and Olivia were living elsewhere. Now that they were here, she hadn't told him why she was on leave these past few months and he hadn't asked. He was preoccupied with the new house, the move back to the city from the west coast, and his new partner, Natalie.

Kes would like to hate Natalie, an elementary school teacher who exuded exuberance and joy and was nauseatingly positive all the time, but she couldn't. Natalie was good to Olivia and respectful and welcoming of Kes. She wasn't trying to be Olivia's mom. Most importantly, Olivia liked Natalie, and Kes trusted her daughter's impressions of people. Still, it had only been six months and they were already moving in together and had returned to be close to Natalie's family, which had brought Kes's family back to her. Maybe she should thank her.

She couldn't blame Henry for taking Olivia so far away. She had let him, but she hadn't understood how long her heart would be severed. Watching her daughter grow on video calls, singing her to sleep on the phone, listening to her stories of people and places Kes didn't know. That was Henry's punishment, but to be fair he had let her back into Olivia's life. She probably had Natalie to thank for that, too.

While waiting for Olivia to find her shoes, Kes told Henry about the boat. Not that it was wrecked, but that she had seen a boat that had reminded her of the ones they saw on their trip to Italy that day they went to Lord Byron's place, Palazzo Mocenigo, and the Bridge of Sighs where they ate fregola and pistachio gelato. He listened with a polite smile. "It's amazing," he said, "how you can recall the smallest details."

Olivia was happy to see her and that brought Kes close to tears. She was still of an age to unabashedly throw her arms around her mom's waist for a big hug. Kes wished she could be that open, that loving and unguarded. They said their goodbyes and headed for school.

Olivia had a new backpack, something they were supposed to go out and buy together.

"I'm sorry I couldn't pick you up last night, sweetheart."

"It's okay, Mama."

"I like your bag."

"Natalie got it for me."

Kes felt that familiar pang. "I don't have a whole lot of time this morning, but would you like to walk through the park on the way to school?"

"Yes!" Olivia took Kes's hand and skipped along beside her. The morning was crisp and smelled of fallen leaves, but the sun was already warming. A perfect fall day.

"Liv, did Daddy tell you Mama was back at work and might have to miss a few days here and there?"

Olivia slowed and walked quietly, swinging her arm between them. "Uh-huh."

"But I'll find other times and Daddy will help us have more times together."

"I like when you're not working," Olivia said.

"Christmas isn't far away now and then we'll have two whole weeks together. Just you and me."

"That's a long time till Christmas, Mama. A whole lot of tomorrows. There's school, there's Halloweens, there's Thankgivings...and a whole bunch more. Daddy showed me the squares on the calendar. You're way, *way* far down the squares."

Kes's heart ached. "I guess it feels like less time when you get older." They walked a bit in quiet. "I was thinking of painting your room for you. What colour should I do?"

"Green!"

"Green! Wow, okay, like the forest or a frog?"

"A forest! With big trees!"

"Growing? Where will I plant them? In the bathroom?"

"No!"

"The closet?"

"No!

"I know...in the fridge."

Olivia giggled. "Silly Mama."

"Oh, I know, I'll just carry them in from outside..." She picked Olivia up in a big bear hug and flung her over her shoulder. "I think this could work," Kes said to gales of laughter and squeals of delight.

She dropped Olivia off at school an hour late. They had stopped to watch the squirrels hiding nuts, which was worth any reprimand.

Kes stood patiently, keeping her body language and face blank, staring at a spot fixed just above Captain Francis's head as he vented his disapproval. She'd disobeyed direct orders to step away from the case. He cited the violations, the disrespect, the liability for the department, for him, the audacity of presenting herself as the officer in charge of the case at the medical examiners...

She stood at attention, hands behind her back, in the glass-walled office for anyone to see. She let her boss's anger envelop her, hot and white. She didn't let it burn her. She listened to the words, accepting them all. She had done these things, but she didn't regret any of it.

When he finally stopped pacing, the Captain sat heavily. She could hear him taking deep breaths to rein in his anger. He wasn't a man accustomed to allowing his emotions to overtake him. In the lull, she took the opportunity to speak.

"With all due respect, sir," she said quietly, "I know there's a connection, and Molly's the key." Only then did she make eye contact. She watched for any tell that would show his hand. "I just want one interview with Molly, sir. In your presence. And if you still think there's nothing further to pursue, I'll tender my resignation immediately." He didn't blink. "But if, after the interview, you agree there's something more to this case, then it's mine."

Captain Francis watched her closely. In the silence, she was calm. If this was where her career ended, she could live with that. She'd rather that than be relegated to cases he thought were safe and unlikely to cause him any strife. She couldn't work caged. She was asking him to trust her. She was asking him if she could trust him.

"I'll hold you to it, Detective."

"I know."

He centred his chair to his desk. "I don't have the legal authority to order Molly to come in," he said. "She would have to do so voluntarily."

Kes assured him, "She'll come."

At five to three, Kes was sitting in the interview room. It was larger than the old station's and air-conditioned. Sterile, bright, modern grey, and designed for easy mop up. Kes had insisted the interview not be done in her captain's office; she wanted Molly to be uncomfortable. Captain Francis joined her at two minutes to three and sat beside Kes in a stiff-backed chair.

"Best behaviour," he said. "This is not an interrogation, but a courtesy."

Again, Kes wondered what his connection was to the Kinder family.

The captain's phone buzzed. "She's here."

Kes stood up and positioned herself in the corner, behind the suspect's chair.

"Right this way." A young police officer gestured to the room and Molly Kinder entered.

"Thank you for coming in, Ms. Kinder," the captain said.

"Molly, please." She offered her hand, forcing him to stand. "Nice to meet you, Captain. My father has spoken highly of you."

Molly sat first, taking the chair directly across from Captain Francis. She wasn't wearing a bra and her legs were bare and her skirt short, despite the fall weather. She ignored Kes completely.

"That will be all," Captain Francis said to the officer. They waited until the door clicked shut. "I appreciate you giving your time to assist us, Molly."

"Any way I can help, Captain, after all this inconvenience."

"That's what we were hoping." The captain smiled warmly. He seemed charmed by the girl. "It's a simple matter, really. Because you were reported missing, we have a few questions to wrap up the report."

"Of course." She leaned back in her chair and crossed her legs.

"How did you get back to the city?" Kes asked from behind her.

Molly didn't even bother to turn around, directing her answer to the captain. "I was walking along the road at the end of the docks and a woman drove by, rolled down her window, and asked if I needed help. I told her I was trying to get back to the city and she said she was heading there herself and graciously offered me a lift and I took it."

"And Lucas?"

Molly dragged her hand through her long hair, sliding it to one side, revealing her neck. The girl was so calm. Kes couldn't see a trace of nervousness. Not a movement of her foot or shift in her breathing. Absolute control.

"It wasn't going to work out." Molly leaned on the table to confide in the captain. She seemed to be enjoying herself. "He's a nice boy, but...you know how that can be. He was too young for me."

"No guilt in ditching him?" Kes slowly stepped forward and stopped in line with Molly's shoulder, studying her profile. "No thoughts as to the emotional and psychological cost to him? He thought you had been kidnapped or fallen into the bay and drowned. He was genuinely concerned for your well-being. He seemed to think you two were in a relationship."

Molly laughed and addressed the captain: "Boys can be so possessive. He knew we were just in it for fun. I'm not one for settling anywhere long." She flipped her hand as if dismissing the absurdity of the idea. "In fact, I had to get back for a date last night. The guy's an ethics prof." She looked directly to Kes. "So I asked him what he thought about what I did to Lucas. Should I feel guilty?"

Kes held her eyes, hid her heart, and matched the coldness of the girl. Hid every tell.

"He said, 'Fair play, equity, and open-mindedness are part of any relationship. Virtue might be too lofty an ideal for mere humans.' He's a bit arrogant that way, but then he's from one of those freethinking Nordic countries. Later, there wasn't much talking." She turned her attention back to the captain. "Handsome man. I like older men."

Kes took the seat across from Molly. She moved with intentional constraint, careful not to scuff the chair leg against the floor. She sat as though Molly had said nothing that mattered. Molly watched her. She was playing a game and Kes was her mouse.

"Do you recall the name of the woman who picked you up?" asked the Captain.

"Something that started with a B, I think. Brenda or Barbara? Maybe Bernice? We didn't talk much. Listened to bad music most of the way."

"What kind of vehicle?" The captain jotted down a note.

"I don't know cars, sir."

Kes watched the tilt of her head and dip of her shoulder which made her appear younger. Practised.

"Do you know a Bertrand Silver?" Kes could feel the captain's sidelong cautionary look to her. She thought she saw a flicker in Molly's eye before she responded. Bemusement?

Molly sat back. "The name sounds familiar, but my mother and father used to have all sorts of people over, so…maybe I've met him. Why?"

"He's dead," Kes said bluntly, and watched the girl's face.

"That's terrible." Molly's words were empty. "It's a dangerous world, isn't it? You never know what's coming."

"Since your parents' divorce, do you see your mother much?" Kes wasn't really sure why she'd asked the question, but ran with her instinct. Molly's eyes changed then, hard and sharp, and her cheeks tightened. A lapse in her control. Kes had finally found a button to push.

"I haven't seen her in a couple years. She has no idea who I am anymore."

"That must be hard." Kes watched for a glimmer of loss in the young woman's eyes.

"We weren't close." Molly turned back to the captain, her features softening again, appealing for his help. "Am I done?"

"Why do you think your father thought you were missing?" Kes said. "He's the one who sent us looking for you, did you know that? Made you a priority." In Kes's peripheral vision, the Captain's foot shifted and his hand tightened on his pen. *Let's see where he fits in*, Kes thought.

Molly looked to her lap. Her hands clasped loosely. Her voice became small and apologetic. "When you come from wealth, I suppose, children can be targets. That's what we were always told. To be afraid. Anybody could grab you for ransom or worse. Father's always been overprotective."

Kes persisted. "You could have called him, let him know you were heading out of town."

"I'm an adult, now. I don't have to check in or report to my father anymore. That's one of the perks of growing up."

Kes could see the shifts of her masks, but hadn't yet glimpsed Molly's true face. *A chameleon*, she thought.

"I'm so sorry my father jumped to conclusions and wasted your time." Molly stood up. This conversation was over. "I think I've answered your questions."

"Thank you again for coming in, Ms. Kinder. My regards to your father." Captain Francis rose from his chair. Kes did not.

Molly smiled sweetly. "Not a problem, Captain."

After she left, Captain Francis sat back down and starting writing in his notebook.

Kes waited impatiently. Surely he could see the girl was lying, unless he didn't want to see it.

He tore out the page. "This is my personal number. Use it sparingly. Senator Kinder is an important man and carries a lot of weight in this city, so the less he finds out, the better for all of us. And if you think I'm trying to cover my own ass, you're correct." He headed for the door. "Lucy will set up what you need. Everything you find comes right back to me. Only me. Understood?"

"Yes, sir."

"Don't ever go behind my back again, Detective." And with that, he left.

Kes stayed in the quiet interview room. Grey on grey. She felt the tremble in the inside of her thigh first. A tremble that carried through her belly, then her chest. She clenched her fist and shook it out. In her heart, a thousand pins needled deeper. *That bitch and Bjorn.*

It doesn't matter, she told herself. None of it mattered. She emptied herself, girded her heart, her mind, felt all the familiar armour snapping back into place. Her mind reeled off all their moments together and apart, looking for signs of his betrayal.

She shut her eyes and let the memories swirl until they blurred into a whirlpool then went black. At the centre was the ache of a pill that could make it all go away.

XV.

Kes drove fast, not slowing for curves, ignoring the ocean slipping past her. She had grabbed her overnight kit, deleted the message from Bjorn on her phone without listening to it, and left a message for Captain Francis: she was heading back to the crime scene and would keep him informed. The Jag slid around a sharp bend and she shifted into higher gear. She had been the only car on the road for over an hour. It was cold and bright, a sharp low sun that hurt her eyes. She was in the barren sixty-kilometre stretch between villages, separated by a hard-scrabble terrain of spruce and bush. The twist and snake of the road added a good half hour of driving time but she didn't want to take the highway. The yellow line whipped past and she rode it tight.

It was easy to imagine when it was just a dirt road and winters cut off this part of the land for months. It was harder to imagine the isolation, when the only way out was by horse or boat. That would have driven her mad. Kes hugged the yellow line around a blind curve and saw a logging truck rounding the bend—too fast, swaying across the line. She veered and her tires fished as she clipped the narrow slip of gravel shoulder. She saw fender, headlight, tires, and the driver's eyes. Scared, too. The truck and its mountain of logs swiped past, and the Jag was buffeted in its wake.

Kes geared down, her hand gripping her father's imprint, and the car settled back in its lane. In her rearview mirror, she could see the truck's tail lights pumping and heard the jake brake thrumming long and low.

A few kilometres down the road, she pulled over at a narrow look-off. She counted the number of yellow leaves left on a maple tree—forty-three—and only then did she look out to the grey-blue water and the hundred-foot drop she was perched on. She could have cried, but she and her sorrows were so small. Betrayed by a man she barely knew.

That's enough, she berated herself. She had a job to do, and a daughter waiting for her. Her time with Bjorn was a fantasy that she had convinced herself was something real. This was what she couldn't explain to the therapists and counsellors: Having a life, letting others in, was dangerous. It made her vulnerable, opened her to mistakes and distractions. She couldn't straddle the world between the living and dead without jeopardizing both. She had to choose. With that she shifted into low gear, looked both ways, and pulled back onto the road.

When Kes got out of her car, Spruce rapped on the fish plant window and motioned that he would be right down. The docks were busy with the unloading of lobster. Kes could see two boats waiting in the bay, having missed the tide to allow them passage into the small harbour. What had looked like a picturesque tourist destination before had transformed into a vibrant industrial hub.

The docks were laden with lobster tubs and ice littered the ground. An enormous man, crammed into a forklift, was speeding up and down the dock, picking up stacks of tubs, turning on a dime, and barrelling into the plant for a few seconds, before emerging empty and heading back to the wharf. She marvelled at the precision and speed of his ballet.

Spruce joined her. "Gladdie said you were back. The first loads are just coming in."

"Good catch?" Kes asked.

Spruce hollered out to a young man on the closest boat: "Lyle, don't be hanging off like that, see the lines behind you?" He turned his attention back to Kes. "Averaging two to three thousand pounds a boat these first days. Push is on to unload before the tide comes back, then they'll be heading out again. You're here at good time. I've got a fella who saw something down at the dock that day. He just got in an hour ago. They're offloading. I'll take you to him."

"Thanks for asking around." Kes thought Spruce seemed strong again.

"Not a problem. Didn't think you'd be back so soon."

"Kind of like your Dumping Day, time is precious with a case," she said. "With every tide, more is lost."

"Or found," he said. "Too bad you weren't here yesterday morning to see this place." His voice brightened. "Everyone was down to wave them off. At ten, the flare fired, and they steamed out together whooping and hollering. A thing of beauty." He was proud of his community.

Kes eyed him curiously. She wondered who Spruce was beyond his job and this wharf. She followed him to a small crew unloading the last of their catch. The low, squat boat didn't have any of the sleekness of a sea vessel. It seemed implausibly imbalanced to ride the waves. "It's as wide as it is long."

"Few years back, government put in a regulation about how long a lobster boat can be, made it impossible to break even with the price of fuel and overhead. But people always find a way around bad decisions made in offices. There's a guy up the bay, cuts old boats in half, right down the middle, then ribs them crossways and fibreglasses the bottoms. They aren't any longer, but they sure are wider. Completely legal, by the way." He seemed to admire their outlaw ingenuity. "There he is. Walter!" he shouted.

A rough-looking, thin man looked up and waved to Spruce. He nodded to Kes and climbed up to the dock. He could be anywhere between thirty and fifty, it was hard to tell.

"Walter, this is the detective I told you about. Tell her what you saw."

"I don't want no trouble," Walter said. "Most things you see out here, you don't talk about. That's the way it is. This is a favour to Spruce, nothing else."

"It's not going to come back to you," Spruce reassured him. "She's good."

"What did you see, Walter?" Kes noted his hands were cut and cracked from years of handling lines. He had dark circles under his eyes and a twitch of his neck that made her wonder if he was on something.

"I was fixing traps down in the pen, and I seen this chick wave to some older dude idling out there in his fancy boat. Then I seen her climb down the ladder on the other side. That's it. Then the boat took off. You shoulda heard the engine on the thing. Sounded like a plane."

"Would you say they looked friendly?"

"Didn't really think much about it, just not what you see in this harbour so much, especially this time of year. Past tourist season and all. Maybe I thought he was her father? She was young and he weren't. That's it. That's all I seen." He looked to Spruce. "I gotta get back. Gotta pull traps while the money's running. We're good, yeah?"

"Thanks," Spruce said. "Stay safe out there." Walter clamoured back down the ladder. Spruce turned to Kes, "Hope that was a help."

"Could be. Thank you."

"I have to get back," he said. "Gladdie's not so good with people." He turned to leave.

"Spruce..." Kes stopped him. "How are you doing?"

Spruce took in the bustling docks. "It's good to be busy. Seems to burn the ghosts out of you."

"It can." Though it had never worked for her. Maybe he would be luckier. Maybe his ghosts would leave him alone.

"Who did we find out there?" he asked.

"I'm sorry, Spruce. I can't talk about the case."

"It'll be up and down the coast soon enough," he said. "I heard Bert took a strip off you."

"Yes, Chief Hawthorn wasn't too pleased with me." She swallowed the desire to defend herself. "He was rightfully worried about you."

"Don't make too much of it. He's got a protective side to him. We were young when we lost our dad. Doesn't matter how old we get, I'll always be his baby brother. Watch your back." He stepped in to guard her as the forklift zipped past. "Docks can be dangerous places. I knew what I was getting into. I thought it'd be the girl we'd be pulling out. Someone's gotta do it, right? Good luck, Detective."

Kes watched him head back to the plant. She sensed someone watching her and looked up. Gladdie was in the window. Kes waved. Gladdie did not.

The temperature had dropped considerably when Kes left the Wheelhouse Pub, and she wished she'd brought a sweater. The sun had just dipped below the horizon and there was a soft pink hue in the sky illuminating the clouds. She took a moment to breathe in the vista before heading back to the motel. Kes wished Olivia could be with her for moments like this. She should bring her here in the summer. Her daughter might not be old enough to remember it, but it could be the start of their adventures together. She hoped Olivia would love the sea.

The only vehicles in the motel parking lot were Kes's and one other truck, but when Kes asked for her room key, Jillie said the motel was full. Extra crew brought in to help for Dumping Week. At Jillie's feet, her little boy was sitting on a handmade quilt playing with little wooden boats. He pushed them through the waves of the fabric.

"His dad carved them for him. That one looks just like ours," Jillie said and handed Kes the key. "The crews will be back at all hours, their trucks can be loud, so I've put you in the end room. It's a little quieter."

The room was identical to the previous one. Kes turned the thermostat up and flicked through the television channels. Her phone chimed. A personal call. She warily checked and was relieved it wasn't Bjorn.

"Chester. You have news?"

"Hey, Kes. A little. I've traced that phone number to Slipaway Travel. It wasn't a main number, but it's linked to a cellphone under the company that belonged to Bertrand Silver. The log shows mostly international calls, Eastern European by latitude and longitude. All incoming. No pattern. Just one call from each number, none of which I've been able to trace. But the last incoming call was local, from a motel on the north shore."

"The Orchard Way."

"How'd you know?"

Kes looked out to the sign, the lights having just come on. "I'm there now. Everything seems to come back to our victim, Mr. Silver."

"I'm still working on the Kinders and any connections with the victim, but there's no red flags on the senator yet, other than some controversial case decisions. Strange, I haven't come across a single mention of his child or his ex-wife in the media. It's like they've been scrubbed."

Kes mulled it over. "Maybe an agreement with the press to keep work and family separate for security concerns."

"Possibly, but there's always bread crumbs. I'll keep digging. I also have an address for you, the maiden office of Slipaway Travel is near you. It started as a small local company before going national."

Kes jotted down the address and pulled up a map on her phone: forty-five minutes up the coast.

"Website lists the business as permanently closed, but the digital footprint indicates that information was recently edited."

"Great work. That should give me what I need to start."

"Kes…" Chester paused like he was choosing his words. "I have ten days of vacation coming up. If you want, I could come and give you a hand? Wouldn't be a big deal and I wouldn't mind the drive."

"Wouldn't you rather hang out at your cabin and do nothing? Have actual time off?"

"It'd be good to see you. I can be there in under three hours."

Kes thought there was more behind his offer, but didn't push it. "I'll think about it and let you know." Her captain wouldn't let her bring Chester in officially, and she wasn't looking for a partner. Mostly though, she was worried Chester would see right through her and ask her how she's been, and she would tell him everything. "Say hello to the gang for me," she said.

After she hung up, Kes sat on the edge of the bed. In her heart of hearts, she would've liked to have said yes to Chester. It'd be nice to have someone she trusted to talk to about the case. Someone who would have her back. Someone who knew her before and would still see her that way. And if she told him about the pills, he might understand how it happened. And wouldn't judge her for failing, like she judged herself.

You're getting soft. It was her own voice in her head.

Get up. She heard Master Jin. *Get up.*

She did a punishing series of kata, until she was bathed in sweat and heaving for breath. If someone had been looking through the window, they would have seen a woman fighting phantoms.

That night Kes dreamed she was aboard a boat. The sea was smooth as glass. Walking impossibly across the water towards her was Molly. In her wake, a massive wave was rising.

XVI.

Down at the wharf, the late morning still held a chill. Kes stood apart from Chief Hawthorn. They had exchanged civilities and not much more. Her captain had called Hawthorn and asked him to provide Kes with whatever she needed, as this was now a murder investigation and she was the lead detective. Her phone buzzed and she checked her messages. Bjorn. Again. *You okay? Getting worried. Check in when you can.* She deleted them all.

Spruce's boat was slowly approaching the dock with a Zodiac following closely behind. Spruce gave her a wave and Kes waved back. Hawthorn looked at her, but didn't say anything. The engines cut to low and the boat sidled in. The tide was high and there was only a three-foot difference between sea level and the wharf. As Spruce's boat turned, the hull of the *No Nonsense* limped around. It was listing heavily, water brimming in its gashed keel.

The entire transom had been chainsawed off and the engine pillaged. All the brass fittings had been pried away and any worthwhile length of mahogany ripped off the deck. Rocks had been thrown through the cabin windows and the once elegant craft was now nothing more than a broken shell. As the remains of the boat slid into dock, Spruce slipped the line and the speedboat eased in, barely nudging the buoys, and sighed into stillness. A teak board had been pried off the stern, altering the boat's name to *No   sense.* Kes thought it was fitting.

"Once the tide heads out we'll load it up, take it to the precinct, and process it to see what we can find," Chief Hawthorn said.

"Too late for that, wouldn't you say? There's barely anything left of our crime scene." Kes wondered why he had waited so long to act. She held his eyes, looking for guilt or remorse, and saw neither, just his swallowed pride. She walked back to her car and didn't look back.

Kes joined up with the secondary highway. The morning news broadcast warned of two escaped cows wandering down Mercy Road. She certainly wasn't in the city anymore. Kes flipped through the stations. Every song—rock, country, pop—was about someone yearning, wanting, bemoaning love. She shut it off.

She crossed an old steel bridge that spanned what looked like a river, but in six hours would be a deep muddy gully. She was still following the tidal basin to the river head. The metal deck of the bridge made a strumming sound inside the car. She passed old farms, car repair shops, and hairdressing salons on her way through what appeared to be poorer communities. No matter how small the village, each had a church steeple visible from miles away. She cut inland through shrub that gave way to fields and vineyards. Acadian flags and stars adorned homes and garages.

She arrived at Little Harbour half an hour later. She marvelled at how distinct and varied the geography was in such a short drive. This was an actual town.

The houses were grand with a Georgian influence, and the fretwork and paint were impeccably maintained. There was an active bank and post office, historic red brick with high arched windows. Down a sideroad, she glimpsed the masts of sailboats in a marina or boatyard. Small boutiques advertising high-end clothing and furnishings were interspersed with fusion restaurants and a craft brewery. She remembered vaguely that the town had once been known for its shipbuilding and gypsum. Now it was a trendy tourist spot. Kes wondered how the town had managed to hold onto its wealth.

On Main Street, she found the Slipaway office, which comprised the entire main floor of a sandstone building. She parked out front and stood before it. A carved keystone dated it 1847. The windows were covered with brown paper. The wooden sign hanging above the door was gilded in gold.

A car drove past with a beagle baying out the back window. It was an unnerving, desperate, piercing howl. Kes watched the vehicle pass, as did everyone else on the street. A man beside her, who had also paused to take in the sight, smiled.

"The hunter," he said. "It must have a scent." He was an elegant man with an upright air. Old-fashioned in his attire. Long wool coat. An accent she couldn't place. "Remarkable how far they'll chase their prey, oblivious to the pain...hunting until they drop. Admirable breed." He nodded goodbye and carried on his way. Kes could still hear the baying dog in the distance.

She checked the travel agency's door. Locked. She peered through its etched window panes. There were a few tables and chairs, posters of exotic places and cruise ships on the walls, and a woman packing up boxes.

Kes knocked, startling the woman, who shook her head and mouthed the words "We're closed."

Kes continued knocking until the woman opened the door. She had a pencil tucked behind her ear. Mid-forties. Tall. Fit. Well dressed. Careful makeup. She carried herself in a way that accentuated her height.

"I'm sorry, we're closed." The woman was composed and businesslike; perhaps she didn't know her boss was dead.

"Detective Kes Morris. Sorry to disturb you." She held up her badge.

"You're here for Bertrand." The woman sighed as she opened the door wider, and Kes followed her in. "He's not here."

A huge antique globe sat in the middle of the room. She could see now that the posters adorning the walls were advertisements of vintage steamship and railroad lines from all over the world. The setting was designed to offer a romantic temptation. In the back of the main room, two packers were taping boxes shut. Kes noted the empty filing cabinets.

"Do you know where he is?" Kes pried carefully, unsure what the woman knew.

"He's deceased." Her eyes welled. "But I'm sure you knew that."

"I'm sorry for your loss." Kes took out her notepad. "What's your relationship to Mr. Silver, Miss..."

"Judy. Nothing. No relation." The woman's face hardened and whatever flash of emotion Kes had seen was gone. "I'm the office manager. I handle day-to-day operations."

"When was the last time you saw Mr. Silver?

"Three days ago." She glared at the packers and the loud squeal of tape unrolling.

"Is that unusual?"

"No, he's not in the office much anymore. He's supposed to be retired, but he still oversees all the branches. He's the boss...was the boss." Her voice trembled. Kes wrote *Mistress?* next to Judy's name.

Kes walked around the room, admiring the posters and taking in the ornate architecture. Even in the process of being deconstructed, it was clear the company had catered to a discerning clientele. "It's a beautiful space."

"Bertrand always said we were selling an experience. Adventure, escape, wonder."

"I understand Slipaway has other offices?" Kes stopped at the massive globe and gently spun it.

Judy looked to the packers unceremoniously stacking boxes. "You need to mark what cabinet they're from." She wasn't accustomed to relinquishing control. She stopped the spinning globe. "We have offices in major port cities across the country. We specialize in cruises. This is the mother company, where it all began twenty-seven years ago by Mr. Silver." Judy paused. Her voice tightened. "And his wife."

"How long have you worked here?"

"Since the beginning. It was my first job."

"And now you're shutting down?"

Her eyes sharpened. "You'd have to ask his wife about that."

One of the movers headed into a side room with a stack of collapsed boxes and packing tape.

"We'll do that room later," Judy redirected him.

Kes walked casually to the open door. "I presume this is Mr. Silver's office?" From the threshold, she looked inside. It was as far as she could go without a warrant or permission from the widow. She just needed to keep the door open and Judy talking. "It's sad to see a small-town business shut down."

"It's like a death." Judy's eyes welled again.

A large map of the world took up most of the back wall and a series of shelves behind his desk were crammed with travel memorabilia. There was an elaborate oversized desk, leather chairs, and banker's lamps. Silver liked to show his wealth. Kes made note of the computer cables and absence of a computer.

"Did Mr. Silver seem worried about anything these past weeks?" On the wall beside the desk was a large frame with two photographs mounted side by side. One of a horse and the other Silver's boat. An engraved plaque on the bottom read, *No Nonsense I & II.*

"No. We were planning a trip to Aruba...he was happy." She wanted Kes to know she and Bertrand were in a relationship. Judy looked to the photographs. "He loved that boat. It was part of him. How could he fall overboard? It doesn't make any sense."

"He..." Kes stopped short; Judy didn't know the manner of death. "I'm sorry, I can't discuss the case with you." Kes felt the sting of the unspoken words: *because you're not his next of kin.* "Judy, where is Mr. Silver's computer?"

"I don't know," she said. But they both knew she was lying. Judy closed the office door. "Perhaps you should contact Mrs. Silver if you have any further questions."

Judy gave Kes directions to Silver Stables and saw her out the door. The lock clicked shut behind her. As Kes headed to her car, a moving van pulled in. Mrs. Silver wasn't wasting any time.

XVII.

Kes was heading back up the basin. The road climbed up a small valley, then through a dense forest that opened onto lush fields before cresting at the cliffs. The bay opened before her. She pulled over on a well-placed look-off and got out of the car. The air was crisp and a breeze lifted from the water. From this vantage point she could see the cliffs tapering off towards the valley, leading to the riverhead, and in the other direction, the view stretching out to the ocean.

It was a stunning vista made more dramatic by a dark bank of fog that sat low over the cold water. She looked for the colourful fish shacks of Spectacle Harbour and the now familiar contour of its bay, only twenty kilometres east, but they were hidden by the jagged coast. Directly across from her was the point where the *No Nonsense* had run ashore.

She got back in the car and notched up the heat. Another kilometre down the road, she turned into the driveway leading to the Silvers' home. White fences enclosed manicured pastures on either side of the drive. She passed two beautiful barns, a riding ring, a gleaming black-and-gold horse trailer, and at the end of the lane she arrived at an impressive bungalow with that modern farmhouse look that seemed to be popular among the rural wealthy.

Kes knocked. A well-kept woman, trim, and wearing expensive riding clothes opened the door. Her silver-blond hair was pulled tight in a single braid. There was no warmth in her smile.

"Come in, Officer. Judy said you'd be here shortly." She wasn't wearing a ring.

"Detective Morris. And you're Mrs. Silver?"

"Billie Silver. Tea?" Billie guided Kes to an uncomfortable settee covered with a cowhide.

"I'm sorry for your loss, Mrs. Silver. I was on the boat that found your husband and brought him back to shore."

"That must have been horrid. It's all been so horrid. Here, take a seat and I'll be right back with our drinks."

Kes watched Billie walk to the kitchen. She looked to be in her early fifties. She had the aura of a comfortable life about her. Wealth and privilege. Kes scanned the room. Everything was richly tasteful. Curated. There wasn't any sense of the personal on display, but the walls were hung with lavish-looking art. Old paintings with gilded frames, like one would expect to find in a museum. On the side tables and mantle were sculptures of horses. Some bronze, some stone. All exquisitely detailed and very old. Kes noted the high-end security system.

Billie returned with a teapot and matching cups on a wooden tray and placed it on the table between them. Across from Kes, a large picture window overlooked the pasture where three sleek black horses nibbled on the grass.

"Beautiful horses," Kes said.

"Friesian, hardly a horse." Billie poured two cups of tea. "What were you hoping to find at the office,

Detective? Maybe I can help you?" She sat with the air of a queen holding court. There was nothing in her presence that indicated a grieving widow, no sense of the fear, pressure, or sorrow of losing a loved one.

"I was hoping to get a sense of your husband. Find out who he had met with recently and where he had been? Do you know if he had any enemies? Someone who he owed money or might have wanted to hurt him?"

"What strange questions. Sugar? Milk?"

"A little of both, please." Kes watched Billie's still, calm hands pass her the vintage teacup. There were callouses on her palms. A rider's hands.

"Bertrand Silver was a big man, in every way. He never did things in half measure. That might have upset some people, made them jealous, but why does any of that matter?"

"Because someone murdered your husband."

Billie took a sip of her tea and stared out the window. Kes wondered whether she was in shock or was actually this cold and detached.

Kes retrieved her notepad. "Do you know Molly Kinder?"

"Peggy's daughter? No, not really. Why?"

"She might have met your husband on his boat the day he died."

"I don't know anything about that," Billie said, as though swatting away a fly.

"Do you know why Mr. Silver was seen in Spectacle Harbour on the day of his death?" She watched Billie's placid face.

"He was always puttering around in that boat. It was his favourite place." She held the teacup in her hands despite the scalding heat. "He loved to be on the move, that man."

"And where did he keep his boat?"

"The private marina in Little Harbour. A small group of businessmen got together, built a seawall and cribs for their boats. I don't go there myself. I prefer the land to the sea."

"And where is this marina?"

"Pirate Lane, they called it. Men will be boys." There was no warmth in her tone. More like disdain.

Kes looked up from her notes. Billie kept herself reined tight. "You said you know Peggy Kinder?"

"Of course. We were part of the same social circle. Not that I liked her much, but I knew her. She always had her nose in the air. Then the divorce and after that... well, another sad story."

"And the senator?"

Billie set down her cup like she was bored. "He preferred socializing with other important men."

"Like your husband?"

"Bertrand kept work and play separate."

"We know that Peggy Kinder took excursions with your husband's travel company..."

"*Our* company," Billie corrected her. "Thousands of people did. I usually stayed here with the horses or went to events with them." She looked out the window at the stallion. "*No Nonsense* was our first stud. That boy out there is his grandson."

Kes didn't follow her gaze. "So, you never went on trips with your husband?"

"Oh, I didn't say that. I went on many of the early ones, when we were building the business. We bought our first horse in Spain, and then I simply preferred to stay home. Better company. People can be nasty. When they travel they want everything different, but the same. The same food, the same luxuries, the same comforts...I grew tired of it. Horses are simpler, more honest. More noble." Billie shifted a pile of art books to align with the edge of the coffee table. "So I made a decision: Bertrand had his world and I had mine. That was our arrangement." She looked to Kes's full cup. "Is the tea not to your liking, Detective?"

"I don't like tea," Kes said.

"Neither do I." Billie laughed. "But it's what people do, isn't it?"

"Did Mr. Silver live here?"

"Most nights." Cool and empty. "Not all is love, dear, but it worked for us."

"And Peggy Kinder? Did she have the same... arrangement?"

"My husband had many arrangements. Would you like to see the barns while you're here? Most do." Billie rose and Kes was expected to follow.

The stallion walked abreast of them along the fence, curious about what they were doing.

"We have three now, but he's the prince. Can't you see a knight being carried into battle by him?" Billie reached inside the main door of the barn and grabbed an apple from a wicker basket. She flipped it to Kes. "Here, give this to him and he'll let you stroke his neck."

Kes held the offering over the top of the fence and the massive beast craned its head towards her and pulled the apple from her hand with its soft lips.

"You mentioned 'events' earlier. Do you race them?"

"Dressage and stud. He's a highly desirable line."

Kes ran her hand down the stallion's neck, surprised at how solid it was. All muscle. Its black coat gleamed. Its long mane and tail had a natural wave. Silky, feathered tufts fringed its fetlocks. It stood easily two feet above her. The horse's eye watched her. She couldn't read what it was thinking. Snorting, it flipped its head and Kes snatched her hand back.

"He won't hurt you. Come on in, take a look around."

"Do you know if your husband ever brought anything back from his trips? Anything to sell? Perhaps on the black market?"

"You ask the most peculiar questions, Detective. Do we even have a 'black market'?" She continued towards the stables. This faux naivete was becoming irritating. Billie was leading Kes around like one of her horses.

The barn was impeccably clean and heated. Stalls with sliding doors lined both sides, and at the far end stood a large hay mow with a mechanical lift. Ribbons encircled the entire stall section, overlooked by an office with a long window. Beside it was an impressive tack room. Billie slid open the huge back doors and light flooded the interior. Beyond were fields extending behind the barn where Kes could see other two horses grazing. Large trees seemed artfully placed in the pastures. A mansion for horses.

"It's stunning," said Kes.

"You can see why I prefer to stay here."

"Do you know where your husband's computer is?"

"Was it not at the office?"

"No."

Billie didn't seem surprised. She reached for a burnished black saddle studded with silver. "I suppose that would be something to ask the lawyers, once you have a warrant. Would you like to join me for a hack?" She gave Kes a cold smile.

Kes smiled back, just as cold. "I should really get going. I may have other questions later. Once I have that warrant."

At that moment, the horse neighed and kicked up dirt as it raced across the field for no apparent reason but the joy of moving fast. Its long tail and mane plumed behind it. Its powerful high-stepping gait was magnificent, and Kes couldn't help but marvel at its beauty.

XVIII.

It was just after three in the afternoon when Kes drove into the Pirate Lane Marina. The clubhouse was a converted boat shed with a deck overhanging the river. The parking lot held a dozen sailboats on cradles that had been hauled out for winter storage. There were a few still in the water, but most berths were crowded with day cruisers. Aside from a few people working on their boats, it was pretty quiet.

Kes walked out onto the floating dock just as a speedboat went racing up the river, the wake rocking the sections of wharf. The small, shallow-keel sailboats swayed in their moorings, their halyards jangling against aluminum masts. A man with a can of varnish and paintbrush in hand stood up on his rocking vessel and shook his fist at the speedboat. "Asshole!"

He was older, mid-sixties, early seventies. Shirtless. Fit. Wore a *Pirate Lane Marina* cap, Sperry deck shoes, and a Rolex Submariner watch. Money. There was a fresh-looking scar on his knee and he was sweating profusely.

"Excuse me, are you a member here?" Kes asked.

"I'm one of the gang who pay a lot of money to tie up our boats here. You visiting?"

"Working." Kes held up her badge.

"You looking into Silver's death?"

"What do you know about that?"

"Nothing." He set down his brush and can. "A boat accident."

Kes suspected he had heard a lot more. "Did you know him?"

"Everyone knew him. The 'unofficial mayor,' or so he liked to think."

"Is that so? Not a fan?"

"He was funny as hell, but I never liked him. New money, didn't know how to carry it. Always needed to show it off. Like that boat of his."

"He kept the *No Nonsense* here?"

"That berth over there." Kes looked to the end of the dock and the empty space. "Ridiculous name, but quite the vessel. Now I hear it's a heap of scrap."

Word was spreading, just as Spruce had warned.

"When's the last time you saw him?"

"Last month, maybe. I wasn't able to get out much this summer. New knee."

"How'd he come into his wealth?"

"Who can say? I just know he didn't have any when he first came here. I remember his father. A mean bastard. They didn't live on the right side of the tracks then. There were rumours the old man was a rum-runner. But people talk when they don't have a story."

Yes, they do, Kes thought. She looked to the narrow river and its muddy banks. "The tide must restrict when you can get in out of the bay?"

"Only at low, an hour either side you're good to go. These shallow keels are designed for these waters. It can get choppy, but if you stay in the middle, between the channel markers, you can get in and out of here most anytime." He looked to the empty berth. "It's a shame about the boat," he said. "She was a fine vessel."

He didn't say anything about the man.

The sun had dropped and Kes swung the visor down to block the glare. Her phone chimed and she held it up to see who was calling: Bjorn.

Her stomach lurched. She tossed the phone back on the passenger seat and swallowed her anger, a bitter mix of confusion and shame. How could she have read him so wrong? She pulled over in front of a church and parked. She rummaged through her notes and found the medical examiner's number.

"Detective Kes Morris calling, I'm wondering if the tox reports are in on Bertrand Silver?"

"Hello, Detective. Straight to it, hey? Yes, we have the results for you. Give me a sec."

She could hear Dr. MacDonald typing. She looked up at the church steeple and a crow perched on the cross.

"Got it," he returned. "Mr. Silver had a trace amount of cocaine in his blood. Combined with adrenaline, perhaps enough to wrench the wheel from the boat."

"Any idea when he ingested it and whether it was administered to him?"

"At least six hours before he died, maybe even residual from the day before. Possibly recreational use, as they say. I have no way of knowing if it was taken voluntarily."

Kes quickly jotted down notes.

"Your victim also had bruising around both kidneys, which I had originally attributed to the fall. But I'm certain now it was the result of two direct blows to the lower back. He was punched hard. Very accurately."

"Like by a boxer?"

"Possibly. Or military. These weren't random hits. They'd be extremely painful, the kind that would drop you to your knees. By the skin discolouration, I would say this happened prior to the victim being bound to the wheel. The rope cuts and bruising around his wrists were fresher, a direct result of him trying to free himself."

Silver was a big man. Fit, athletic. Whoever overpowered him was strong. Cocaine wouldn't have subdued him, it would have amped him up. Molly couldn't possibly have felled him. Unless she had assistance?

"I can also confirm the toothmarks belong to a tiger shark. Incredibly rare in these parts. There's only ever been four sightings." He sounded excited by this discovery. "The victim would have bled out from the femoral artery before the frigid waters could take him. He would have gone fast. Unusual there was anything left. Tiger sharks don't pull off like great whites when they realize they've made a mistake. They'll eat anything, even a cow carcass has been documented." He had been doing his research. "Regardless, your victim would have succumbed to drowning or hypothermia had the shark not bumped into him. He was a dead man the moment he hit the water."

Crows cawed overhead. Kes could see two birds squabbling around the steeple. They hooked claws and plummeted in a churn of feathers and wings. She watched them freefall, waiting for one to let go. To her shock, they hit the ground. The strongest kept attacking and others swooped in. Pecking at its head and chest, yanking on feathers. And then they were gone. The dazed and battered loser stretched its wings and flew off. Kes looked up to the murder of crows now perched on the steeple.

"Detective? Are you still there?"

XIX.

THE NEON ORCHARD WAY SIGN LIT UP WHEN KES PULLED IN. There was a note stuck on her door: *I'm in room 6. Is there a good place to eat around here? Chester*

Kes was surprised by how thrilled she was he was here. A solid guy, someone she trusted. A friend. She walked down to room six and knocked. Chester swung the door open.

He grinned sheepishly. "Detective Morris!"

"Chester. Quite a surprise." They didn't shake hands or hug. There was no proper way to greet each other.

"You never know where a vacation wander will take you," he joked. "I hope it's okay?"

She could use his help and, truthfully, she wanted his company. "It's so good to see you again, Chester. I'm taking you out for dinner, my treat."

"Great. I'm famished and I have beers in the cooler for dessert."

Chester still had that grounded presence of someone who worked on the land. He hadn't physically changed much since she last saw him. A few more lines around his eyes. His hair still in need of a cut, but he had lost the scruffy goatee. She noticed the nicks on his knuckles and the callouses from working with wood. His eyes were bright and he seemed genuinely happy to be here. She wondered why he had really driven this far to see her.

Kes and Chester sat by a window overlooking the bay. They had finished dinner, fresh lobster cooked in sea water, and were nursing their third beers, having caught up on police news and gossip, circled around the weather, spent some time talking about an expansion to the cabin and a new wood stove. Kes kept diverting the conversation back to him. Superficial conversation, pleasant, but they had reached the pause that indicated they had run out of common knowledge because they were colleagues, rather than friends.

"What else is on your mind, Chester?" Throughout the meal, he had seemed distracted, as if waiting for an opportunity to speak freely.

"I've been offered a job as Head of Information Technology at a private company in the city. Security. Global."

"Leave the police force?"

He looked down to his beer. "It pays well. Really well. I'd be set."

"But...?"

"I'm not sure what side I'd be working for. Global security can get murky. And I'd have to move."

She couldn't imagine him separated from the woods.

He picked at the label of his beer. "And I have a girlfriend now. Her name's Grace." He smiled. A goofy, tender smile.

"Congratulations! Grace and Chester. I like the sound of that." She wondered what kind of gal had picked him. She imagined someone playful and strong. Someone who could bridge head and heart with ease. So why was he here then, rather than with her?

"You shouldn't have come, Chester. You have more important things in your life now." She didn't want to bring him into another brutal investigation. She could still recall the look in his eyes, seeing the horrors of the Holy Cross case. He should go home and have a shot at a normal life.

"I wanted to talk to you, Kes, a woman, not just a woman, but someone who understood..." He was tripping all over himself. He took a breath and tried again. "I don't have sisters and my mother died when I was a kid, so family's out. When you called, I thought..."

"Do you love her?"

"Yes." There wasn't any hesitancy. "Absolutely."

"So what's the matter?"

His leg was bouncing under the table. "Three days ago, she told me she's pregnant." He looked up at Kes and smiled with a shrug. "We're pregnant."

"That's good news, right?"

"Yeah..." He didn't sound as certain. "I never saw myself as a father. I was happy on my own, but now..."

"I think you'll make a wonderful father, Chester." And she did.

"Father. Right? Such a big word. Mine ran off. Never knew him. Not really sure what the job is, you know? I don't want to screw it up." He said this like a vow. "You have a daughter, right?"

"I do." He was asking her as a friend. "She's five now. Olivia." Saying her name made Kes uncomfortable. She kept her daughter apart from her work. Not many knew her name, but she trusted Chester.

"I want to get married, but the cabin's no place to raise a kid. They could have so much more in the city."

"Maybe, but what will that do to you?"

"Does that matter?" He looked directly at her, expecting the truth.

Kes chose her words carefully. "I don't know if you can deny part of your heart without it costing you something."

"If it's better for them, for my child...I don't think that's even a consideration. I would happily give pieces of myself for them."

Chester was a good man. Young in his conviction. Who was she to tell him about heartbreak and failure? If anyone could make it work, it was him.

"And I love being a cop. But that's hard, too. Hard on families. How do you do it?" he asked. "Hold the job you do, and the things you've seen, and not bring it home? How do you separate yourself?" He swept the shreds of the beer label into a mound, pulling all the pieces into a tight ball.

"I'm not the right person to be asking, Chester. You should be talking to Grace."

Chester looked up at her. "She said I should talk to you."

He knew her as his boss. He knew nothing about her as a person. "Chester..."

"Grace is great and she's proud I'm a cop." He needed to get it out. "But she can't really understand what we do. I don't tell her about the worst days. I don't tell her everything. Being a cop means that will always be between us. How do you protect them from that?"

Kes wanted to tell him that it didn't have to be that way. She wanted him to believe he could have a good life beyond the job. That he could make it work. "All you can do is try to give your family a safe place to land." She tried to hold back the emotion creeping up her throat. "Give them laughter, be there for them, don't stop talking. Don't look away. Don't ever forget what you have together."

She wove the story he wanted to hear. Everything she didn't do. Everything she wished she had done. Everything she wanted for him.

She couldn't tell him how she had failed Olivia. How she played that day over and over. Found excuses. She was sleep deprived. A new mom back at work. Her father had just died. Mother, wife, grieving daughter, detective. No excuse. She couldn't tell him she had given up Olivia because it was the only way she knew to keep her safe. And that somehow her sweet, sweet girl had forgiven her, or forgotten, when she couldn't forgive herself. Or forget. Who was she to give advice? She couldn't tell Chester any of that.

"You'll do your best," Kes said and clinked glasses. "That's all any of us can do."

He reached across the table, took her hand, and squeezed.

She squeezed back.

XX.

AFTER DINNER, THEY WENT TO CHESTER'S ROOM, WHERE HE had set up his office. Kes had given him one more chance to bow out, but he said if he took the job offer on the table this could be their last case together and he didn't want to lose out on that. When he called Grace to let her know he'd be a few more days, he handed the phone to Kes so they could meet. Grace sounded like Kes had hoped. Funny, smart, lively, open, and in love. Grace had only one request: "Send him home safe."

Chester had brought a six-pack of craft beer with him and Kes was on her fourth of the night. She was perched on the bed, her back propped against the headboard, reviewing her notes under the dim reading lamp. The only light on in the room. Chester sat cross-legged on the floor hunched over the low, round coffee table crowded with his laptop, hard drives, compact projector, printer, and a slew of cables. Kes brought him up to speed.

"Silver had trace amounts of cocaine in his bloodstream and bruising to his kidneys, which is likely what allowed him to be overtaken. I don't think Molly's capable of blows like that. And he was tied to the steering wheel, forced into that position. That takes strength."

The wall had become an impromptu screen and images Kes had sent Chester filled the dim room:

closeups of Silver's wrists, the snapped steering wheel, the severed limb.

"Molly's lied about everything, but that doesn't mean she killed him. And then there's her father, who sent me on the hunt for her in the first place...the senator. Garreth Kinder."

Chester opened files on his computer. "Yeah, I've tried to find more on him. Nasty business when he doesn't get his way. I've located his ex, Peggy Kinder, who kept her married name. Currently residing at Willow Glen, a care home just outside Little Harbour. This is the most current photo I could find and it's from seven years ago."

The image spilled over the wall. A black-tie event, Peggy standing beside her husband. The senator shaking hands with someone outside the frame. Peggy staring blankly in the other direction.

"How old is she now?"

"Fifty-eight."

"In a care home?"

"A private care home. It seems someone's paying that bill. The divorce was brutal. She got a hundred grand and that was it. His firm came out swinging, but I can't find out why she accepted such a low settlement. Maybe he had something on her?" He took a sip of his beer.

"Do you have the address?" Kes's phone vibrated and the address appeared on her screen. "Can you be faster next time?"

He laughed. "I'm just warming up." He closed the images and the wall lit up with dense, scrolling code and a map pinging around the world. Stockholm, New York, Shanghai.

The beer was getting warm and Kes was tired. "I went to Silver's place of business today, Slipaway Travel. There was no computer in his office. His widow, Billie, was a cold piece of work. Said I had to talk to her lawyer. Can you find out who that is? She owns Silver Stables. Raises horses..." She checked her notes. "Friesians."

"That's an expensive habit. Let's see." Chester's fingers flew across the keyboard and his expression changed to one of total concentration. He seemed as bright and focused as if it were the top of the day. The hunt was firing him up. Kes checked her watch: 10:45 P.M. She used to have the same endless well of energy. "You're being careful, right?" she cautioned him.

The map was pinging on the wall, every few seconds.

Chester laughed and pointed to the map. "We're in Zambia now, oh Wichita...I close my back doors, Kes."

Kes didn't understand this new world of technology. She was being left farther behind with every software update and technological advance: AI, ChatGPT, social media forensics, facial recognition technology, intelligent surveillance systems. Even Olivia could create her own games on the computer with singing dogs jumping over barrels and dancing on their hind legs. But Kes had been trained to read people. To look into someone's eyes, to watch their breath or the twitch of their cheek, to feel whatever was hiding inside. Technology couldn't be taught to feel. It didn't care about the victim. It was never haunted by what it saw.

"Got it!" Documents flitted past faster than Kes could read them. "Billie Silver sold a horse last year...one hundred and seventy thousand dollars. A grandson of *No Nonsense*. The sale was handled by her lawyer, Robby Klein. Just a second." Chester broadened his search.

"You're going to like this: Robby Klein of Sawler, Kinder and Klein."

"Kinder." They clinked glasses and Kes finished the last of hers. She hadn't lost her instincts. They *were* connected. Billie and Molly had lied. Kes was wide awake now. Ready to hunt.

Chester grinned. "What a tight web we weave." His tone turned serious. "You know they're never going to let you look at Silver's computer. Even with a warrant. It'll get lost or they'll claim it was stolen."

He typed in a code that shuddered his screen black. The room dimmed. "Turn your phone off." Kes complied. His voice lowered. "This is confidential, okay?"

"Of course." Chester's eyes, which had seemed so boy-like moments before, now held the serious, careful man he was. Someone who knew more than he let on.

"When I was a kid, sixteen, seventeen, I was a white hat. Used to hack into companies, big ones. I loved the game of finding my way past their security gates. There's always a mistake somewhere. A door left open, mail from a personal account, a drop unprotected. Average people don't know the risk. Employees, home computers, sharing memes, clicking links…a thousand ways to get in. When I'd crack it, I'd send the company an email letting them know."

"Jeezus, Chester."

"They always freaked out. I'd usually hear back a few hours after they reviewed the code and they'd ask what I wanted."

"Which was?"

"Nothing. Just wanted to show them it could be done. That was the thrill. I'd also tell them how to fix it. They never believed my motive. They'd offer money, non-disclosure agreements, anything I wanted. Some threatened prison, but they didn't know where I was. It was exciting." He leaned in closer. "You know most companies backup to a cloud. It just takes one window left open. Kes, you have me for the week."

"Chester, you know I can't authorize any of that."

"No, you can't." He leaned back and finished his beer. He smiled. "I'd have to be a ghost."

Back in her room, Kes stretched out on the bed and tried to quiet her mind with the TV on mute. She scrolled through the channels—fifty-two—three times before she turned it off. It was just after midnight and the night made her restless for the day. She thought about Chester and fatherhood and the corpse and how life could simultaneously be so unpredictable and so beautiful and so horrible. You just had to find your way around it. *Through it*, she corrected herself. She opened up a picture of Olivia on her phone and propped it on the pillow beside her.

"My girleen."

Kes shut her eyes and she was right back to that day. She didn't try to push it away. She let it play like she always did. Olivia, not yet a year old, asleep in the back seat. Driving in circles like her dad had done with her. The stop sign. The van blowing through. The child killer they had been chasing for months. He had looked right at her. That face. She had interviewed him three times, couldn't hold him, and he'd disappeared. And here he was, right in front of her.

She didn't hesitate. Didn't think. Called for backup. Did everything right. Multiple units responding. Two squad cars intercepting. The turn. The guardrail. The van. Flipping. Only then did she pull over. Officers, weapons drawn, one shot. His. She watched them drag out the lifeless body. Only then did she hear Olivia crying. Only then did she realize what she had done.

Kes opened her eyes and touched the photo of her beautiful girl. She didn't try to stop the tears. This pain was her punishment.

Kes woke late. Her mouth was dry. She was still wearing her clothes from the day before and hadn't even bothered to slip between the sheets. Apart from her overnight bag in the corner, the room was as tidy as when she'd first arrived. She liked to live small when she travelled, preferring not to leave any piece of herself behind.

The shower was weak and tepid, but it still felt good to wash away the four beers she'd had last night. Too many. But it was an unexpected night of camaraderie.

She looked in the tiny mirror above the sink. *Don't lie to yourself*, her eyes stared back. She had liked creeping up to the edge again. The dulling of everything. That would have to stop. She had a small nagging headache behind her eyes and slurped a handful of water from the faucet. Then she called Olivia and made her voice bright, even though she hadn't had a coffee yet. The pain moved to a dull throb behind her left eye.

Olivia told her about the highlights of her previous day, especially about a boy named Roger who peed down the slide. She had a new French teacher, Mr. LaPointe, who'd had a long moustache that looked like a caterpillar and he could roll his Rs a long, long time. After five minutes, her dad called her for breakfast and Kes remembered it was the weekend. "Au r-r-r-revoir, Mama," Olivia said and left the phone hanging when she ran off to the kitchen. Kes heard Natalie ask her, "How's your mum?" and the line disconnected.

In the distance, Kes could hear church bells, her weekly reminder of what a heathen she was. She sat for a moment mapping her day, replaying the night's session with Chester. She needed to interview Peggy Kinder. Her phone pinged. Chester: *Mean anything to you? Grabbing some sleep.*

Good, she typed. He'd been up all night. Heading to see Peggy. She opened his attachment:

Lozenetz	*2*
Vlorë	*1*
Pukë	*2*
Osijek	*2*
Zadar	*1*

The words and numbers continued for two full pages. *Names? A list of scores from soccer teams in Europe? Or hockey?* She had been told Silver was a betting man. Maybe this was insider information from a bookie? Only one word had a vague impression, *Zadar*. She entered it in her phone and searched.

A town in Croatia. Now she remembered why it sounded familiar. Olivia had told her about the Sea Organ she had learned about in school. The tide played it. They had watched a video and giggled that the ocean wasn't a very good musician. But Olivia had insisted Kes just wasn't listening properly.

She typed in the first word on the list. A town in Bulgaria on the Black Sea. She carried on down the list:

two others in Albania, also on the water, and the next in Croatia. She opened a map and searched for the towns and their proximity to one another. All were in Eastern Europe, more specifically The Balkans. Most could be reached by boat, either from the sea or by rivers. Were these cruise destinations? But former Eastern Bloc countries didn't strike Kes as typical tourist fare.

She texted Chester: *Towns. Eastern Europe? Soviet Bloc?*

Her phone rang. She picked it up without checking caller ID.

"You're supposed to be sleeping," she said, expecting Chester's laugh, but there was only silence.

The line was open. She checked the ID: *Unknown.* She brought the phone to her ear and listened. The caller hung up.

XXI.

THE WILLOW GLEN CARE HOME WAS INLAND, BUILT ON farmland. Massive willows canopied the yard with paths and benches scattered throughout. There wasn't a soul in sight. The building was long and low, painted a sallow yellow.

Inside, Kes was greeted by an empty front desk. An awful floral watercolour featuring birds and rabbits hung on the wall behind it. Sage, lilac, and dusty rose, all of her most detested colours. A young man in a crisp white shirt and navy vest with a willow stitched over the heart came from behind the venetian blinded window in the back office. He looked more like a concierge than a care worker, with the exception of his black canvas sneakers.

"Help you?"

"Detective Kes Morris. I'm here to see one of your patients."

"We refer to our guests as clients or residents. ID?"

Kes held up her badge. "And your name?" she asked, as he squinted to study it.

"Matt."

"And what do you do here?"

"Personal care worker."

"Matt, I'm here to see Peggy Kinder."

"Is everything okay?"

"Police business."

He looked at her quizzically. "I don't see how she can be much help."

Kes clipped her badge back onto her belt. "If you could just show me to her room. Thank you."

Kes followed Matt down the beige corridor. Cheap, banal landscapes lined the hallway. She could smell sickness and disinfectant as they passed closed doors with interchangeable nameplate holders. There was nothing hopeful or comforting anywhere. A vase of fresh-cut flowers in the hallway would have been the least they could do. And it was quiet. Too quiet. Like everyone was asleep in the middle of the morning. All she could sense was emptiness, and it made her feel queasy. They reached a door at the end of the hallway and Matt knocked gently.

"Peg, you have company." He pushed open the door, then stood back to allow Kes inside.

The room was dark and it took a moment for her eyes to adjust. Peggy Kinder was sitting in an easy chair staring at the dim light coming through the trees. A wall-mounted TV was on mute, some morning talk show. There weren't photos or anything of Peggy's family or previous life on display. Nothing of the past.

"Hello, Mrs. Kinder. My name is Kes. I was hoping to ask you a few questions."

"Hello, nice to meet you." Peggy smiled warmly. "I'm Peggy." She was wearing an oversized bathrobe and a mismatched top and pants. Lavender and green.

"I was hoping to ask you a couple questions about your ex-husband, Garreth Kinder, and your relationship with Bertrand Silver and Slipaway Travel."

"Of course. *Bertrand*. Bertie. He should use sunscreen, you know. I always told him that." Peggy was still smiling at her.

Kes eyed her curiously. This was the woman photographed in a silver evening gown, champagne glass in hand. "Bertrand was a friend of yours, Mrs. Kinder?"

"I'm Peggy," she responded. "Nice to meet you."

"I'm Kes." Whoever Peggy Kinder was before, she was no longer. "I understand you used to travel? With Bertrand Silver. Do you remember any of your trips?"

"Oh yes! The buffets were wonderful. I was always seated at the captain's table."

Perhaps some of Peggy's memory was intact. "Do you remember where you went?"

"Everywhere, darling. Life jackets are stowed at the bow and aft. Women and children first. Will you be joining us for the buffet?"

"No thank you, I'm good." Kes tried another approach. "Your husband, Garreth, worked with the Silvers on a regular basis..."

"Garreth? I don't know that name. Is that someone I should know?" Distressed, she looked to Kes. "Am I supposed to know him?"

Kes could see a flash of the woman trapped inside. "No. I'm sorry, I must have the names mixed up."

Peggy looked visibly relieved. "I thought so. I never forget a name."

Kes wasn't going to find any answers here. "I should be going. Thank you for your help."

"Don't forget to sign the guestbook."

Kes smiled back. "It was nice to meet you, Peggy."

"Nice to meet you, too." Kes could hear the lilt of her previous wealth and privilege. She turned to leave.

"Have you seen Molly?" Peggy asked.

Kes stopped. "Excuse me?"

"Molly. Naughty Molly, always sneaking out to be with her friends. Daddy's girl." Peggy's eyes blankly shifted to the TV screen and she seemed to fade. "I'm very tired. You should go now, Molly. I'm not hungry anymore."

Kes stepped into the hall and Matt closed the door.

"Is she always like this?"

"Pretty much. Some days are better than others. This is a good day."

"What's wrong with her?"

"I don't think I can share that information. Client confidentiality. I'd have to get my supervisor."

"That won't be necessary." Kes deflected to keep him talking, pulling up the few facts Chester had found. "She's been here five years now... Any visitors? Family, friends, her daughter..."

"No, none that I've seen. Sad, but not unusual. We do our best to keep our clients happy."

"Expensive to stay here? All this care. My mother may need help soon, what would that set us back?"

"Five to six thousand a month. Financing is available."

"Thanks, Matt, you've been very helpful. If anyone comes to visit Peggy, I'd like you to contact me." She handed him her card.

Matt looked pleased to be invited in. He checked the card. "You're from the city? Homicide?"

"That's confidential." She forced a smile on her way out the door.

Kes sped back to the motel, opening up on every stretch. The care home and its heavy weight of sadness and mortality had distressed her. She tried to outrace the irrational dread and fear prickling under her skin. Peggy was only fifty-eight. A disease, a hit on the head, a bleed in the brain. That's all it took. Or one bad call…or a car crash. Kes slowed and focused on the road.

She could look at corpses and feel nothing, but couldn't bear to look in Peggy's eyes. Someday she would have to instruct Olivia to never let her end up in a place like that. No, she wouldn't put that burden on her child. Kes turned up the music, Beth Hart's howling vocals, and loudly sang along until even the case quieted in her mind.

XXII.

Kes's motel room had been cleaned. She noticed her sweater was draped on the desk and the bed covers had been smoothed. She looked to her bag on the floor. Nothing out of place. It always unsettled her knowing someone had been in her room. There was a knock on the door and Chester entered with his laptop in hand. He walked past her, jumping right into the case.

"I've been working on that list. Some in Croatia had KBC or KB in front of the name. In Croatia, those letters refer to a clinic or hospital. I went through the list again with that in mind and there were places with hospitals by the same name. In Dubrovnik, Croatia, there's a Dubrovnik Hospital. In Põlva, Estonia, the Põlva Hospital..."

"What use would a travel company have for hospitals?" She'd missed this exchange of ideas with a colleague. "They could be hotels? The Hotel Dubrovnik, or Hotel Põlva?"

"No, no matches for hotels." Chester plopped down in the only chair. "And not restaurants, sports fields, post offices, or museums, although museums were the closest."

"If they're hospitals, it could just be a list Silver kept in case of emergencies, if one of his travellers got sick?"

"Maybe, but usually when people travel they're heading to escape reality. Australia, the States, Europe, UK, whatever southern island, sure, but these are all in Eastern Europe, countries that in the nineties were still in the throes of recovering from political, social, and economic collapse. And then there's the numbers. *Dobrovnik 2, Põlva 2, Merkur 3*. It's unlikely three people went into the Merkur Hospital on a single trip."

"That's still assuming the code is referencing hospitals." Kes sat on the bed.

"But it's giving us something to circle around." Chester was excited. "I kept going and once I got past the emails and travel confirmations, I found a correspondence drop between Slipaway in Little Harbour and its city office. Someone attached a photo of a dog to the file with a stupid meme, which let me into the financials. I narrowed the search to the names of the towns—"

"Chester...should you be telling me this?"

"Probably not." He changed track. "So, I was walking around and I found right there in the middle of the road..."

Kes smiled, willing to play the game.

"...all the records for the last twenty years, when the company went digital. The first seven years of paperwork weren't uploaded, but these show typical expenses you'd expect running a travel agency, except in the periods right before and after trips to the locations on our list: expenditures and profits significantly increased. Unlike their more typical, sunny tourist destinations."

Kes proceeded cautiously. It was so easy to go off trail. "But it could also just reflect client costs for more off-the-beaten-path adventures. More to organize, visas, insurance, bureaucrats to pay off, higher risk? Not necessarily a red flag."

"Sure, but this one is in Bulgaria. Before the country's fairly recent independence, it was a satellite of the Soviet Union and had its own Communist government." Chester brought his laptop over to Kes and pointed to the list. "This one's in Estonia. It, too, has a long history of being dominated by other countries and was a union republic of the former USSR. And these ones are in Czechoslovakia, Hungary, Romania, Albania—poor countries all once part of the Soviet Bloc. All with ports. Beautiful places, sure, but who would've taken a vacation cruise there twenty years ago in that chaos?"

Kes listed the possibilities: "Arms dealers, drug runners, traffickers, smugglers…"

Chester sat back. "And Slipaway Travel."

"And Slipaway Travel." Kes flipped open her notepad to the branching names of *Bertand, Billie, Molly, Peggy,* and *Senator Kinder*. "So, why kill Silver? A business deal gone bad? They could have thrown him overboard and mocked it up as an accident. It would have been simpler, cleaner. But this kill was brutal and personal. And how does Molly play into it?"

"Maybe she doesn't."

Chester was right. Never make assumptions. Hadn't she taught him that?

"Dig up everything you can on the Silvers and Molly, whatever footprint they've left behind. See if we can link them. Can you pull together a chronology of the trips?"

"Not a problem. I'm going to try to dig up the manifests, too."

"And anything more you can find on Peggy Kinder. Who pays for her care?"

"Copy, boss."

"Chester..."

"Sorry. Copy, Kes."

"And can you send me the address for Slipaway's city office?"

Her phone pinged and Chester winked.

The parking lot was full of pickups. Spruce's old boat was tied up to the dock, but all the others were out. Kes looked up to the large window on the second floor of the fish plant, but couldn't see Gladdie. She pushed open the warehouse door and smelled brine and lobster. A tractor trailer was being loaded at the back and workers dressed in long white coats, hairnets, and rubber gloves were packing banded lobsters on layers of crushed ice. No sign of Spruce.

"What you doing, missy?" an older man hollered from the line. "This here's private property."

"Looking for Spruce."

"Out back."

Kes waved her thanks.

A hundred metres behind the warehouse was a jumble of storage sheds and a Quonset-style structure, which she guessed had once housed a metal fabricator. Along the side of the building was a pile of welding cable, an old rusted Esso sign, and a small heap of twisted metal. Spruce was nowhere to be seen. Kes peered through the green-tinted window. It was surprisingly tidy. A row of tools pegged to a wooden workbench, a pair of overalls, and one large shiny engine suspended above the floor on a chain hoist. Spruce stepped out from a side door.

"Surprised to see you, Detective. What're you doing here?" He pulled out a cigarette, lit it, and stretched his back.

"Looking for you."

"Found me. Good timing. I was just taking a break. How are you?'

"Good, Spruce. Thanks. You?"

"Living the life." He smiled, but it had none of the warmth she expected. "What can I do for you?"

"I know there's a long history of illicit trade on these waters. From privateers to rum-running."

Spruce laughed. "Sure, we've got buried treasures, ghost ships, and headless ghosts, too. Good stories for cold winter nights."

"Some are more than stories, Spruce." He was keeping her at bay and she wondered what had caused this shift. "You know these waters and I suspect you have a good sense of most everything that goes in and out."

He shrugged. "I've seen some things."

"I'm wondering how the drug runs work."

"You should be asking Bert about that."

"I'm more interested at a practical level," Kes said.

"I've heard stories like everyone else. I don't know nothing personally."

"I understand," she reassured him. "This is just between you and me."

He eyed her cautiously, unsure of her motive. "There's tankers and cargo ships coming through here all the time. Mostly farther up the bay. Coming from Venezuela and them parts. Maybe they're carrying oil or some kind of cargo in. I hear things fall overboard sometimes, and boats like the one we found, fast little boats just happening by, might pick those things up. And from there, who knows where they land or what they're doing." He was being cagey.

"Law of the sea?" Kes said.

"That's right."

"Spruce, I'm not interested in who's doing the pick-ups. I'm not looking for names. I'm tracking the murder."

He took a long drag of his smoke, considering his answer. "There are things that aren't talked about here. Not good for your health. Especially when my brother's the chief of police. It's none of my business. I keep to my own affairs."

"What do you know about Slipaway Travel?"

"It belonged to our dead guy. Didn't know it was him when we pulled him out. He was quite the piece of work."

"In what way?"

"He came from a long line of bad. Big shot, or thought he was. He used to throw parties at his horse ranch. Girlfriend of one of our guys worked one. Big tips. Powerful men. Lawyers and politicians. Cuban cigars, Caribbean rums, coke. I used to hear a boat out on the bay some nights, sounded a lot like his engine. Never saw it, though, so I can't say if it was or wasn't. You gotta wonder how he made all his money."

"You hear anything about his wife, Billie Silver?"

"The horse lady? Snotty. If he was the king, she was the queen." He carefully stubbed his cigarette on the ground, then put the butt in his pocket. "I have to get back."

"You do engine work, Spruce?" He looked at her guardedly. "There's grease on your hands."

"Yeah." He rubbed his hands on his pants. "You have to know the basics if you have a boat."

"This your place?"

"Yup, it's my hut. Good place to get away with friends some nights. Play cards and whatnot."

"That's a nice-looking engine you have hanging up in there, but I'm not going to ask you about it. Law of the sea and all." The engine from Bertrand Silver's boat wasn't her concern, but she wanted him to know that she knew.

Spruce nodded, maybe acknowledging that he had been caught, but there wasn't any regret in his eyes. "You know there's sheds and barns and tables made from salvaged wood up and down this coast. There's an outhouse with portholes and a mermaid figurehead in the community hall. My grandfather was said to have Captain Kidd's desk, but he was quite the storyteller."

He looked to the bay. "You know, I got back out on the water the other day, first time since that night. Never been away from her that long," he said. "I think it's going to be okay after all. It's still the same water, like you said." He considered the engine his compensation. "Good luck in your hunt, Detective Morris. But it kinda sounds like Silver was playing in dangerous waters. It's been nice meeting you."

Kes watched him amble away. She had read him as an uncomplicated, easygoing man. What you saw was what you got. But he was also an opportunist without any moral qualms in taking what he saw as his right. And this place...She looked to the plant and wharf beyond. They all knew what was in that shed. He didn't get it in there alone. She had been charmed by Spectacle Harbour's beauty and hospitality, but it had been a siren's song, which made her question what else she had gotten wrong.

XXIII.

The ducks were asleep and Kes could make out their slumbering forms in the dark pond. She shifted in the large Adirondack chair and slowly sipped a lukewarm beer. The night sky had cleared and beyond the row of motel porch lights and row of expensive trucks, Kes could see the stars. She looked back to the motel. All the rooms were dark, except for the soft glow behind the closed blinds of Kes's room. An empty pizza box sat outside the door. Chester was still working.

At first, he told her what he was doing: trying to find an access point into travel manifests, working through digital footprints for Molly, the senator, Bertrand, and Slipaway. The deeper he went, the more technical his descriptions became, until he stopped talking and lost himself in the screen. He didn't notice when she stepped outside for air to keep herself from falling asleep.

It was chilly and Kes wished she had brought a heavier sweater. She curled her legs up under her, pulling her sweater over her knees, and looked up to the swirl of the Milky Way.

She marvelled at the millions of stars visible. All this was lost in the city. She could locate Ursa Minor and Major, but all the other stories of crimes and punishments of vengeful gods and goddesses eluded her. She fought back a yawn. She was tired and embarrassed that Chester could outlast her. That wasn't like her. She wasn't fully back. Her mind was foggy, her senses dull. Maybe she had taken on too much too fast. Or she was just tired of all the dead ends of this case. She was lost in the woods. Her father would have told her to stop running then. *Retrace your steps. You always leave a track if you look carefully enough.* The woods were thick. Brambles tore at her legs. There was a trail ahead. She didn't know if she was dog or human or something other. She could hear the pant of her breath. She was on a scent. She pushed through the bush and there was a pond of sleeping ducks. She inched forward silently, her muscles tensed, coiled to pounce. She woke to Chester laying a blanket over her in the chair.

"It's late," he said. "I tried to wake you, but you were dead asleep."

Kes looked to the pond and the unperturbed ducks. Puzzled. "They're still alive."

―――

Kes and Chester met at the small highway diner up the road for a late lunch. The cheap laminate tables and plastic flowers in old bottles made her worry about the quality of the food. Faded photos with handwritten captions adorned the walls: *Buddy Jones holding up a teacup found in lobster trap*; *Ms. Penelope's class of 1905*, and the like. There was a baked goods stand and behind the counter were displays of local crafts *Not For Sale*.

They ordered the all-day breakfast special and were delighted to be served farm-fresh eggs, local bacon, homemade bread and baked beans, and never-ending refills of coffee. Only the coffee didn't meet the diner's exceptional standard.

Between bites, Chester updated Kes on what he had found. "I checked Willow Glen's accounts; I tell you these private care homes have no security, a three-year-old could walk into them. I had to leave them a message. Haven't done that in years."

"Chester!"

"They can't be that careless with personal information. It's important they know. Ordinary people have no idea how vulnerable they are and nobody's going to tell them. Most don't even update their software. They might as well leave their front door open with a sign on it that says *Come and Get It!*"

Kes could imagine her colleague as a teenager, hunched over his computer in his bedroom. He must have been an odd kid. "The case, Chester."

"Five thousand dollars every month is deposited into the care home account to cover Peggy's costs. And I found her personal account offshore; that wasn't easy, I'll tell you."

"Don't tell me," Kes implored.

He spun a story for her. "Right, so there were some documents in the trash I happened to see… Peggy Kinder made sporadic deposits to an overseas account over the years. Some up to fifty grand. Quite a few of them. They didn't come regularly, and some years more deposits were made than in others. Her balance is just over half a million. The account hasn't been touched in five years."

"So, ever since she got sick. Who's paying for the nursing home, her ex? The senator?"

"Funny you should ask. Slipaway Travel. From a miscellaneous account in Bertrand Silver's expenses. The payments are made out for PK Consulting. There's no record of a business by that name, but every withdrawal corresponds with deposits to Willow Glen."

"Why would Bertrand Silver pay for Peggy Kinder's care?"

"He owed her?"

Kes thought back to the photograph of Peggy and the senator at the party. Who was she looking to just outside of the frame? Maybe it wasn't boredom in her expression, but yearning, a silent exchange. Billie said the Kinders had known each other for years and that she didn't like Peggy. She didn't mention that the senator had been their company's lawyer or that their connections went back much farther than a few social encounters. Peggy must have been one of Bertrand's *arrangements*. Is that what dissolved their relationship?

Chester sopped up the yolk with his bread. "I still can't find anything on Molly Kinder. I swear it's like she's been scrubbed. If she's leaving a print, it's being swept up. I've gone back as far as her birth, Central Hospital, but I can't get the file. I don't know if it's locked, if there's data corruption, or if the hospital is just lagging in transferring their archives to digital...but I'm not done yet."

The restaurant door swung open and six raucous, elderly women all wearing purple dresses and red hats stormed in. A table had been set up for them and they noisily took their seats. The server brought coffee for two of the ladies and said she'd be back with teas for the others and their regular orders were in with the cook. The group was loud, boisterous, and out for fun.

Chester grinned. "I hope I'm that spry and joyful when I'm that age." He pushed away his empty plate. "I was talking to Grace this morning. She's feeling good, no morning sickness."

"Lucky." Kes had been lucky, too. She had craved tinned smoked oysters. Half a dozen cans a day. Henry hated the smell.

He looked to the red-hat table. "I could see her dressing up like that someday when we're old and have grandkids. Holy crap, I could have grandkids! You could have grandkids!" They looked at each other, trying to imagine that future.

"You really do love her, Chester."

"I really do." She saw that flash of a small boy in him again. She envied him that love and her mind flitted to Bjorn.

Kes excused herself to go the washroom. Inside the stall, she could still hear the women laughing. She admired their ease with each other. She wondered what her face would look like at that age. The age of a grandmother. She tried to recall the age of her own mother now. Sixty. Sixty-two. Younger? A woman who had never known her own granddaughter, or her daughter.

A loud gale of laughter rose again from the dining room. Kes smiled softly into the mirror as she washed her hands. Thin lines showed around her eyes. Some of the women out there must have lost husbands and children, lived through terrible losses and heartaches, and they were still laughing. She had to remember to laugh more.

When she returned, Chester was checking out the pies in the display case. "I'll take a slice of coconut cream, too," he said to the server carving a mountain of lemon meringue. "A treat for later," he beamed.

"One bill," Kes pointed to herself.

"Aren't they cute?" one of the red hats said and the entire table looked over.

"Well done." Another red hat winked to Kes. Chester blushed.

By the time they got back to the motel, a soft drizzle was falling. Chester headed to his room to continue his research and Kes left for Silver Stables. She had some questions for Billie.

XXIV.

The grey wet made the fall colours pop. This was her favourite season. Life and death in tandem. Kes rolled down the window a crack and breathed in the sweet earthiness of cleared fields and the faint smoke of a wood stove. She turned up Sticky Fingers' "Bootleg Rascal" and the wipers slowly kept beat. She figured she was about thirty minutes from the Silvers' farm.

Billie had lied about her connections with the Kinders. Did she know her husband was paying for Peggy Kinder's care out of company funds? If so, was that enough motive to kill? A murder-for-hire? What did she have to gain? Control of the company, all the assets, her freedom.

The song's beat ebbed and flowed. The wipers scraped against the windshield and Kes flipped them off. Maybe their "arrangement" wasn't as mutual as Billie made it sound. The old cliché of a woman scorned.

Her phone rang. Bjorn. It to get it over with. Life moves on. She turned off the music and hit speakerphone.

"Morris." Her voice was hard and she didn't try to soften it.

"Kes. It's Bjorn."

"I know."

"I've been trying to reach you."

She let the silence sit.

"What's going on?" he said. "Is everything all right?"

She kept her voice emotionless. "Your name came up in a police interview..."

"My name? How? Why?"

"A student." She could see a steeple in the distance, stark white against the moody sky.

"Who? About what?"

"I can't say." She wanted to hurl the name *Molly Kinder* at him. "She said you two were dating. She implied more."

"What the hell? Never! I swear to you! When was this supposed to happen?"

Kes spied an eagle and focused on it, so as not to feel anything else. "The night I left the restaurant early." She would like to be sitting across from him to read his eyes.

He sounded truly outraged. "Who made this accusation? I have a right to know who's threatening to destroy me!"

"That wouldn't be ethical, would it?" She held herself back; she wanted to rip him apart. She wanted him to hurt.

The phone went silent, and for a moment, Kes wondered if she had lost the connection going over the hill. Her heart was pounding.

He sighed and his voice softened. "No, it wouldn't be." Before this happened, she had thought Bjorn's integrity was his honour. "After you left that night, I took a cab to my sister's. I stayed the night with her. We were in contact with the hospital in Copenhagen, where my mother has been admitted for pancreatic cancer. It's spread. I was trying to contact you to let you know I'm leaving for Denmark tomorrow. My sister and I want to be with her. I'm sure you have the means to verify my story. Perhaps you'd like my sister's number or the doctor's...? I assume you can access my phone records."

Kes had been had. She'd walked into a trap, because she hadn't trusted him. Hadn't trusted her own instincts. Because she hadn't considered Molly could be that cruel. Kes slowed and pulled over. The engine hummed. Her heart slowed, until she could no longer feel it inside her. "I'm so sorry, Bjorn." She held the steering wheel tight.

They sat in silence.

"I don't know where we go from here," he said. "How could you think that of me?"

She couldn't say, *Because it happens all the time. Because this is what I'm trained to expect. The worst. The worst in everything.* She had nothing to say that could make this right.

After hanging up, Kes immediately called the restaurant. How had Molly known she and Bjorn were together? The only time they had been out since she'd been on this case was that night at the Trattoria.

Thomas answered. They had a security camera at the entrance aimed at the dining room. Kes said she needed to look at the footage from the night she was there. He said he'd check, but he'd have to wait for his son. He was the only one who knew the machines.

Kes asked that the file be sent to directly to her. She fabricated a story about looking for a missing person who may have been at the restaurant that night. She gave him her cell number and thanked him for his assistance. She emphasized the need for discretion; he wasn't to speak about the case with anyone. When she hung up, she tried to work the kink out of her neck. Her teeth and jaw were tight.

How could she have fallen for Molly's lie? Because her heart got in the way. She had let herself care for someone and it had blinded her. Molly knew Kes had a weakness and she had exploited it. Why? To distract, to redirect, to piss her off? This was exactly why Kes couldn't have a real life. She always had to be a cop.

She jammed the gear shift and squealed back onto the road.

Approaching Silver's driveway, Kes had to slam on her brakes when she came face to face with a muddy pickup hauling a horse trailer. It was taking the corner wide on the way out, so she reversed and pulled onto the side of the road. The driver, an older man wearing a ball cap, gave a finger wave when he cleared and accelerated down the road. Kes watched him disappear in the rearview, beyond the bend.

She pulled up the long winding drive through the sentry of trees and parked next to the barn. The black-and-gold trailer wasn't there. She got out and breathed in the damp fall air. The rain had made the ground soft underfoot. The horses weren't in the paddocks. She would have liked to have seen the horses again.

Kes went to the house and knocked on the door. All was quiet. She walked around the side and looked in the large picture window. The walls and mantels were bare.

"Shit." Kes ran to the barn and pulled open the doors.

The stalls were empty. The saddles, tack, and awards: all of it

Gone.

XXV.

Kes slowed as she approached another sideroad, keeping an eye out for the truck and trailer that had pulled out of the stables. She was on the phone with Captain Francis.

"We need to put an APB out for Billie Silver, sir. She's on the run. She has her horses. Alert border crossings, ports..."

"On what grounds, Detective?"

Kes knew she didn't have a case to hold Billie. Nothing tangible to link her to the murder. All she had were theories. "Their company was dirty. Slipaway showed massive profits over the decades that were not typical for a travel agency. They were making multiple trips to former Eastern Bloc countries. Maybe they were involved in smuggling drugs, artwork, booze... And the senator was the Silvers' lawyer in the early days of the company. Molly, the senator, Bertrand, and Billie are connected. I just need more time to link them."

"And how has this information come into your possession, Detective?"

They both knew she couldn't answer.

"She's running, sir. I flushed her. If we lose her now, we lose whatever ties them together." There was a long stretch of silence and Kes wondered again if she had lost the line.

"You've given me nothing to warrant picking up a grieving widow and you know it. Don't pretend otherwise." The Captain sounded tired. "Everything you've said so far is completely inadmissible and likely illegal. You've offered nothing that implicates Billie Silver in her husband's murder. We can't act on your hunch, Detective. I want you to come back and we'll review options."

Her tires hummed across the metal bridge. She could see Little Harbour's church spire.

"I can't do that, sir. I'm so close."

"That's an order, Detective. You did your best. Come home."

Again, Kes felt a nagging doubt that he was protecting someone, or himself.

"This is bigger than our scope, Kes." He sounded almost like a friend. "We have to hand the case over to the appropriate departments."

"It's still a murder case, sir."

"And you've done your part. I'll see you in the office tomorrow morning." He hung up.

Kes drove another kilometre, the autumn colours whipping past. She felt like crying. This was how it was going to end, being pulled off the case like a rookie? What choice did she have?

Up ahead, she saw another crossroad. She glanced to the dirt road sloping over gentle rises and in the distance, cresting a hill, she spotted the trailer and pickup. *To hell with the consequences. This is my case.* She pulled off fast and was soon behind the trailer.

The truck slowed to let her pass and the driver waved her around. Kes pulled up beside him and waved him over. She held up her badge. The truck came to a careful stop and Kes tucked in behind it.

She got out of her car and walked up to the driver's window. She could hear the snort and restlessness of animals inside the trailer. The driver had the look of a farmer. Weathered skin and rough hands. A worn flannel coat and a tractor logo on his cap. Country music was playing low on the radio.

"What can I do for you, Officer?"

"You just came from the Silvers' place?"

"I did."

"What was your business there?"

"Picking up a horse I bought."

"One of the Silver horses?"

"That's right."

"Was Billie Silver there?"

"No, ma'am."

"Do you know where she is?"

"Nope. Just know she's selling off the farm. There's a machine sale next month, but I hear she's keeping most of the good tack. I was hoping to get a saddle for the ones in back."

"You have one of her horses?"

"Two of 'em. Mares. I hear she kept the stud. She didn't want these two parted. They're for my daughter. She's loved those horses since the first day she saw them. Never could afford one, but Mrs. Silver let 'em go for a price I could pay. A gift, really."

"Why would she do that?"

"I've done work for her over the years. Helped with haying, plowing back fields...we help each other 'round here. I think she knew they'd be well taken care of. Not everything's about money, you know." To prove his ownership, he added, "I've got the paperwork on 'em." Like she had accused him of theft.

"Do you know when Billie left?"

"A while before I got there. Horses were watered, fed, brushed. Even had lavender oil rubbed in the halters."

"Lavender?"

"Keeps 'em calm on the drive. She thought of everything."

Kes slowly pulled onto Little Harbour's main street in the vain hope that Billie was still close. She stopped in front of the Slipaway office and saw it now had a *For Lease* sign in the papered windows. Beyond town, highway exits branched in every possible direction. She had lost the scent. She pounded the steering wheel and swallowed a guttural howl that made her throat raw. Silent even in her fury. She thought about the baying dog. What had that man said? They chase their prey until they drop. Kes had always been that dog.

She picked up her phone and called Chester.

"Hey, boss—" Chester stopped himself. "Sorry, Kes... have you tried the chowder at the tavern? I booked us a table for—"

She cut him off: "Billie Silver is on the run, Chester, and taken her prized horse with her."

"What the hell?" His voice lost all its boyish play.

She had already lost too much time. The evening light was falling. "How would she get them out of here, Chester, if she was leaving the country?" She could hear him typing quickly. She loved that he understood the urgency without her having to explain.

"Plane would be preferred. But there's no carrier here handling livestock cargo, she'd have to head to Toronto for that kind of specialized transport."

Kes considered the likelihood of Billie heading cross-country. "No, it would have to be something closer and faster to disappear... A ship? Something she knows."

"It says here that's the next alternative, but not ideal because it's hard on the horses. They get seasick. Who knew? But where could she board around here? Is there a port?"

"There has to be something," Kes said. "Freighters travel these waters."

"There's nothing this side of the bay...no wharves big enough for a ship like that. I'm looking at satellite images—wait..."

Kes could hear him breathing.

"I've got it! At the end of the basin is an old gypsum company that had docking facilities for ships. It's been shut for over a decade. There's a pier still standing. I can see it on the map."

"That has to be it." Her hand went instinctively to the gear shift. She could feel a spike of adrenaline. "I'm in front of the Slipaway office, how do I get there?"

"Okay, just before the turnoff to the new highway. By Strawberry Park. The province turned part of the mining facility lot into some kind of a picnic park when it shut down. You're about forty-five minutes out."

"How high's the tide right now?"

"I'm looking..." She heard Chester typing furiously. "Coming up. It's almost high tide now. I'll meet you there. Don't go in without me." He hung up.

He knew she couldn't promise that. She jammed the car into gear.

XXVI.

Night was falling fast. The sun had already slipped behind the cliffs across the bay. The closer Kes got to the water, the thicker the fog became. Her headlights bounced along a narrow road. For the past few kilometres, the shoulders of the secondary highway were skirted with low mounds of dirty white gypsum. It had to be close. The road climbed sharply and suddenly a sign announced *Strawberry Park.*

Kes veered into the gravel parking lot and stopped at the edge of a well-manicured field with picnic tables and a baseball diamond. At the far side of the diamond was a high, rusted razor wire fence and through the trees she could see the roofs of squat, long buildings and towering above them a metal trestle craning towards the bay, but no apparent way to get there.

Damn it. Kes swung around, spewing stones, and sped back looking for an entrance. The Jag hit bottom and she winced. When she reached the highway, she turned left and slowly retraced her path. She spied a heaving overgrown asphalt road with an unhinged gate.

Kes drove carefully along the road, trying to avoid the larger potholes. Rounding a bend, she was met by an empty guardhouse and a weathered sign—*Safety Record: No. of Days Accident-free.* It was riddled with bullet holes. The fog flared in her headlights as she passed beside a derelict warehouse tagged with graffiti, most of the windows broken. It was coated with thick grey-white dust. Ahead were massive piles of crushed gypsum, hardened into its own mountain range.

Kes rounded the corner of the building and looked up to the trestle crane. She could now see that it was a massive conveyer belt spanning a concrete pad. The underpinnings were corroding and there were rusting footings of dozens more that had once been there. She slowly drove over the snake of railway lines shunting through the lot. *No Trespassing* signs and warnings dotted the fences. Behind her, an industrial light pole flickered and switched on, blazing the gypsum hills bone white. Kes braked. She looked to the row of lamps, most with shattered housing. Only one other, nearer to the water, had come on. Still functioning, responding to the fading light.

Kes followed a narrow lane leading to the bay. Alongside her, washed out dirt roads criss-crossed the marshland. Ahead, timber poles that had once been wharf footings jutted askew from the water. Some snapped, all twisted, their massive wharves sheared away by storms and tides. Kes had been wrong. There was no way to dock here.

Fog wisped and swirled in her headlights. She rounded the last bend and was met by a chain-link fence with metal gates and beyond it a concrete pier still intact. *That's it.* There was a way. She hadn't been wrong. Kes switched off her lights and turned off the car. She rolled down her window and listened. Not a sound.

At the end of the pier, a mercury vapour lamp shrouded by the thick fog cast a dim, eerie blue-green cone of light. Sharp against the night. Looking down the bay, Kes could see the faint lights of a freighter. *Where are you?* She stared at the light pooling in the lot, and the pulse of the fog, and a brief shimmer of gold. And then she saw it at the edge of the light. Sitting all alone in the middle of the pier was the black-and-gold horse trailer. Kes had her.

Her mind raced. It would be at least another ten minutes before Chester got here. Kes couldn't let Billie Silver get on that boat. She was the link to solving this. If Kes couldn't keep her from boarding, she would at least need to find out where Billie was headed and have her picked up at the other end. Maybe if she called Chief Hawthorn, he could hold her on charges of illegally transporting a horse, or trespassing—that was something they could hold her on.

Kes was grabbing for anything to keep the case alive. Spruce had said with the tide they only had three hours to load or offload. She looked out to the bay. The freighter's lights were closer. A bright beam, blooming in the fog, flashed three times in her direction.

She called Chief Hawthorn.

A young man's voice answered. "He's off duty." The officer sounded like he was eating.

"I need you to get him on the phone for me."

She could hear him swallow. "Is this an emergency?"

"Tell him Kes Morris called and to meet me at the old gypsum dock."

"Do you want to tell me what this is—"

"No," Kes snapped. "Get your boss and get him here now!" She hung up and got out of the car. Chester would be here soon.

A large chain held the main gate closed, but on closer examination the lock was unclasped, and the rusted chain was simply draped through the fence. Kes pulled it through the gap and pushed open the gates. She walked towards the horse trailer. The air was cold and fog kept rolling in, tamping the sound, creating a dead, muffled silence. The mist dampened her sweater. Again, the freighter flashed a light three times. Kes cautiously approached the back of the trailer. She stepped wide to check the cab, but the truck was empty. She could hear a low buzzing.

She looked around the dock and back to the building, but there wasn't any sign of Billie. Headlights swept the factory road. She could hear tires on gravel coming fast. Chester. The closer she got to the back of the trailer, the stronger the sound of buzzing.

Kes pulled down on the door lever and slid back the locking bolt. It opened a crack, the humming now a low-pitched frantic buzz. An overwhelming scent of lavender. She swung the door open wide and stepped back. She couldn't see inside. She looked to Chester's vehicle arriving and waved him in, guiding him to shine his headlights on the dark trailer.

Chester flashed his high beams, *Copy*, and sped through the gate. He pulled up and positioned his car so the lights illuminated the horse trailer's interior. Kes held up her hand, *Stop*, as she backed away from the trailer. He got out, leaving the car running, and she motioned him to move slowly and quietly.

Bees churned in the trailer. Thousands of bees. Some spilling out, caught in the light.

"Jeezus," Chester said, taking another step back.

There was a horse lying on its side panting, blood running from its mouth, its hind leg twisted, stuck in the trailer's vent opening. Kes could see a sharp fragment of bone sticking through its hind fetlock. The animal was wall-eyed, its matted black mane splayed around its body. Its sides and flanks were welted with stings. The trailer's wall was heaved and dented outward from its kicks.

Behind the horse, jammed against the wall, a woman's body lay face down. The skull caved in by what must have been frantic hooves. A pool of dark blood seeped around her head, mingling with the glass shards of a vial of lavender oil and dead bees littering the sawdust floor.

Near the open door was a wooden box with mesh walls and a hole in the top. Part of the box was shattered and splintered. Near the horse's head was a crushed empty tin can. The perfect size to plug the hole. Bees writhed over the mesh, some still trapped inside. A *Live Bees* sticker was partially torn off, the shipping address obliterated.

"Is it...?" Chester breathed.

Kes nodded. "Billie Silver." She headed to her car.

"Where are you going?" The horse's laboured breath echoed in the trailer. Its foreleg involuntarily pawed at the floor.

Kes opened her trunk, retrieved her service pistol from its lockbox, and popped in the clip.

Chester watched her return. "Let someone else..." he said quietly.

But she couldn't, and he understood.

"You should turn around," she said.

"Kes..."

"It's easier if you turn around," she said. "Please."

Chester did as she asked and covered his ears. Kes stepped towards the trailer and took aim through the storm of bees. The animal, that gorgeous animal, watched her. A bee stung her arm, then another, and one her neck. She didn't flinch. Her hand was steady. She drew an imaginary line joining the outside corner of each eye with the base of the opposite ear. She pointed her 9mm just above and took aim directly down the neck. Just like a buck hit by a car. Just like her father had taught her when he answered that off-duty call.

"I'm sorry," she whispered, and pulled the trigger. The sound boomed across the bay. She stood there until the horse's muscles stopped contracting, and its body relaxed, and the ricocheting echo was swallowed by the fog, and the ringing in her ears faded, and she could only hear the drone of bees. She reached in and gently touched the membrane of its clouded open eye. No response. She locked the gun's safety.

Kes walked to the end of the pier. The freighter had turned. They must have heard the shot. She could see its red running lights. It was heading back out to sea.

Chester joined her. They stared out at the blackness.

"Should we call the RCMP to try to intercept it?" Chester asked quietly.

"I'll take care of that." Kes breathed in the salt night. "You have to go home now, Chester," she said.

"I want to stay and see this through."

"That's an order. Go home to Grace and your baby. If you're going to do what's best for them, you have to be able to walk away."

She looked at him, her eyes hard and insistent. "You walk away now."

They both understood, *While you still can.*

XXVII.

AFTER CHESTER LEFT, KES WAITED IN HER CAR AND STARED AT the back of the horse trailer. A black pool stained the dock. She didn't turn on her headlights. She didn't want to see that anymore. She closed her eyes and breathed deeply. In her mind, she watched the trailer arrive. Watched Billie get out of the truck and check the bay. Saw her gather up the vial of lavender, walk to the trailer, unhitch the door, and speak soft words to her prized horse inside. The horse unsettled, but trusting. The smell of lavender soothing its fears. A few drops on a brush, running through its mane. Billie ignoring the horse's swaying rump and low snort—sensing you. *You.*

Kes slipped deeper inside. Male. Why male? She reached deeper. Stalking. Calculating. Empty. Approaching from the other side, hidden by the open door. A box in hand. Kes could hear it humming. Him listening to the soft coaxing sounds of a woman who only loved horses. Not caring that both will die. Stepping forward. The horse's ears pinned back. A brief moment seeing Billie, lavender oil on her fingertips, and her seeing him, a silhouette at the door. The can pulled like a grenade and the box tossed in, door slammed shut, locked, and the bees rallying to save their queen.

Him standing outside. Not walking away. Listening until it was over. Leaving not a trace behind.

You wanted her to suffer. Did you regret not being able to see it? Or was hearing it enough?

In a flash, Kes was inside the trailer. Horse rearing, glass shattering, slammed into the wall, the smell of fear and pain, hooves pounding metal, and the horse, the horse, its eye staring at her the moment she pulled the trigger...

Kes pulled back into herself. She gripped the steering wheel until she could see only night and fog coning around the street lamp. Only then did she let herself cry.

Chief Hawthorn arrived twenty minutes later to find Kes sitting in her car in the dark. Music playing. Otis Taylor singing the blues. She shut it off when he approached and rolled down her window. The fog had retreated to a soft haze.

Hawthorn was wearing a fisherman's sweater and sweatpants. "What's so urgent you called me here on my night off? I don't work for you."

Kes didn't acknowledge him. "Billie Silver is dead. She's in the trailer with her horse. I put it down."

"What?" He looked to the trailer, cloaked by the night.

"Billie was leaving the country, meeting up with a freighter here. I thought you could find a way to hold her until I figured out who or what she was running from. But someone got to her first. Tossed a package of bees in and locked the door. The trailer is swarming, warn your team when they go inside. The freighter is maybe an hour away by now, I assume you can coordinate with the RCMP to board it."

"On what grounds?"

Did he not hear her? Did she have to outline every step of his job? "What was it doing here? What do they have on board? Where is it from? Where is it going? What was Billie Silver's arrangement?"

Hawthorn let her tone slide. "Did it dock?"

"No, I saw it coming in and then it turned back. But it was coming for her."

He looked to the dark bay, not a vessel in sight. "Maritime laws are different, Detective, we need a reason to board. You said it was heading out, that it didn't dock...hell, from here you may have seen it leaving from across the way, just following the shipping lanes. A foggy night plays tricks."

Kes's jaw was clenched. "It was coming in. It signalled for her."

"You can't prove that." Hawthorn softened his tone. "By the time we have warrants and jurisdictions are sorted out, it will be entering international waters. We can't touch them. Can't board them. Can't detain them. We have a victim right here."

"Sounds like you want them to get away." The bee stings on her arm were on fire.

"I didn't say I wouldn't try, but the chances are shit. I have to follow the law, Detective." He stood taller, a chief reprimanding an officer. "Something you seem to have forgotten."

Kes started up the Jag and turned on her headlights. The back of the trailer lit up and they could see the horse and pooling blood and the churn of bees. "I haven't forgotten anything. I'll leave this with you. I have to get back to the city. See that she gets there."

"Detective." Hawthorn sounded tired. "We're not enemies."

She looked up at him. His face was taut and his eyes pained, locked on the grotesque scene. He looked older than the last time she saw him. Everything in his manner suggested he was a man telling the truth and doing his best in a situation that didn't make any sense. In that moment, she saw him as a fellow cop who had been at home, maybe watching TV, his feet up, grateful for another quiet day, and then she had called him into this.

"Are you going to be okay?" she asked.

He looked to her, his guise slipping back into the mask of a man who was accustomed to hiding his emotion. "Yeah, I'm good."

Kes put the car in gear and expected him to step back. Hawthorn rested his hand on the door and leaned in. "How are you, Detective?"

"Same as you, sir." Kes softly smiled and pulled away.

Portishead was playing on the car stereo. Kes advanced the tracks until she found "Glory Box." She turned it up loud. The yellow centre line barrelled past. She sped by night convoys of long-haul tractor trailers carrying goods to grocery chains and retailers. The song rose and fell, pulling her into the broken, barbed voice. Hers was one of the few cars on the highway. She passed the airport turnoff and her mind flickered to Bjorn. He would be leaving for Copenhagen soon. The guitar wailed and crunched and the keyboard trilled into a grinding discord, before falling to the singer's sneer and heartbreak. Honest and raw. Something she and Hawthorn couldn't share.

When the song ended, Kes realized she was going thirty over the speed limit. She shut off the radio, sat back, and gave herself over to the pull and purr of the engine travelling through the dark, like it knew where it was going.

It was past midnight when Kes opened her front door. The house was quiet and she felt the relief of arriving. She kicked off her shoes, tossed aside her kit bag, and checked the fridge. The leftovers had spoiled and the vegetables were wilted. She was out of eggs and the milk was expired. She ignored the beer and instead went to the sink and filled a tall glass with water and downed it. She was exhausted. She didn't turn on the hall light and tripped over Olivia's car seat on the way to the bathroom. She didn't bother brushing her teeth. She stripped, tossed aside her bra, kept her underwear on, and curled up in bed. She pulled the duvet high around her neck and snuggled into the pillows. She wondered how long it would take to fall asleep. Her breath rose and fell. She let herself drop into the pitch black.

The water gently rose and fell. It was dark. She was swimming in the ocean, with no land or lights in sight, but she wasn't afraid. Her stroke was rhythmic and strong. Effortless. There was a faint humming. She stopped, treaded water, and lifted her head to see if she could identify what sounded like bees, but the air was thick with fog and she couldn't see beyond the rolling waves.

The noise was getting louder, a metallic grinding roar, and seemed to be coming towards her. The vibration made her neck tingle, and pulsed through her body. The ocean foamed and roiled and then she saw it:

bearing down on her was the bow of a ship. She dove deep.

All around her the buzz of propellers sliced the water above, the droning sound pursuing her. Her lungs constricted. And there in the depths, galloping towards her underwater, was a black stallion. Its mane and tail fanning around it. Its deadened eyes clouded.

Kes woke gasping for air. Her heart thrumming. Her skin clammy. She checked her phone: 2:00 A.M. She counted to seventy-nine before her breath calmed and she could no longer see the horse's eyes.

She pulled on a T-shirt and headed to the kitchen. She stepped up on a chair, reached into the back of the top cupboard, and retrieved a jar. She climbed down, opened it, dumped the old screws and nuts onto the counter, and fished out the small baggy of three white pills.

She nudged one out. She stopped. Her finger on the pill. The floor was cold under her bare feet. The stove clock light was flashing. Kes slid the pill back into the baggy. Stuffed it in the jar, swiped the nuts and screws back inside, and tightened the lid.

XXVIII.

Kes was seated in Captain Francis's glass office. She focused on a smudge on the table. The captain had received the reports concerning Billie Silver's death From Chief Hawthorn and she had updated him on her suspicions that Slipaway Travel and the victims were involved in some sort of a smuggling ring. He turned another page of her file, which now held transit routes and bank statements.

"...and this information you found how?"

"Online." Which wasn't really a lie.

"Twenty years of ships and ports of entries into Eastern Bloc countries...I didn't realize you were that proficient with digital forensics." He glanced to her and waited for an answer.

"I don't understand the question, sir."

"Yes, you do. Have you been working alone?"

Kes wanted to trust him. "I may have had some assistance, sir. Off the books. I needed someone invisible and discreet as per your directive."

He tossed the file aside. "None of this admissible."

"Bertrand and Billie Silver are dead, sir. They owned Slipaway Travel. The senator was their lawyer. He knew their business. He knew what they were hiding. He helped them hide it. His daughter, Molly, who *he* sent us to find, was the last person seen with the first victim.

The Silvers and the Kinders were involved in something together. I want to know if the senator was involved enough that he could be the next target. Or if he or Molly are behind this. We need to bring him in for questioning. I need to be in the room with him."

"You don't have any evidence, Kes. You don't even know what you're chasing."

"A murderer, sir."

"Do you realize what this will trigger?" Captain Francis rubbed away the smudge on the table with his thumb. "You will tread lightly," he warned.

"Yes, sir."

"The vessel you had Chief Hawthorn pursuing entered international waters early this morning. He was refused a search warrant for insufficient evidence. He fought hard to board it. Woke up three judges in the middle of the night. I took their calls afterwards. Hawthorn wanted me to tell you he did everything he could."

"I was hard on him, sir. I'm sorry." He had done his best and she again hadn't trusted his motives. She was pushing everything into the grey.

"Everywhere you go, mayhem, Detective." The captain returned to the file.

"Is that all, sir?"

"Make sure you put in for your ghost's hours and expenses," he said without looking up.

Kes and Captain Francis were seated at the boardroom table when Senator Kinder was shown in. He was short and balding, expensive suit, Italian leather shoes, alumni ring, manicured nails. Head tilted up, chin out, ready for a scrap. A man who expected respect and didn't like to be challenged. His comportment reminded Kes of a bulldog. She couldn't see any of Molly in him.

Kinder dropped his briefcase on the polished table and took in the view of the harbour. "Damn. You cops are doing mighty well for yourselves. Mighty well."

"Good to see you, Senator." Francis rose and offered his hand. Kes did not.

"Don't start this off with bullshit, John. You aren't pleased to see me any more than I'm pleased to be here." He took a seat across from them, scraping the chair across the floor.

Captain Francis sat, brushing off the slight. "Sir, this is—"

"I know who this is. Kes Morris." He eyed her. "Last week she was asked to do a simple job, now look at this mess."

The captain continued with his best diplomatic poise. "You know why we've brought you in, Senator, off the record…"

"Because Billie and Bertrand Silver are dead and I'm on record as their lawyer more than ten years ago. So, no, I don't know why you've called me in for this. I'm here out of respect for you, John, and to close this once and for all."

"We appreciate you coming in, Senator," Kes interjected. "We have some questions about your work for the Silvers." He seemed surprised that she was speaking to him, like she was beneath his status.

"As you know, attorney-client relationships are confidential. We won't be talking about that," he said, shutting her down. "This is a complete waste of my time, John."

The captain sounded conciliatory. "We're hoping you can help us out. It will be brief, I'm sure." He looked to Kes. "Detective Morris is lead on the case and as chair of the Review Board, I know you have a vested interest in solving these murders as quickly and discreetly as possible. We don't want the media drawing their own conclusions." The remark was pointed. The captain leaned back like they were old friends chatting. "Only what you feel you can share."

Kes opened her file and pulled out a page. "Sorry for your loss." He didn't respond. "According to these documents, Billie and Bertrand started Slipaway Travel twenty-seven years ago. You were the lawyer who helped them set up their business. Correct?"

"You already know that." Kinder was accustomed to controlling a conversation.

"Yes, we do." Kes smiled. "I'll cut right to it. What was your ex-wife's relationship with Slipaway Travel?" She watched his eyes. Saw them harden. He smiled back; he had played this game a thousand times in court and the political arena. He liked the game.

"Peggy was a client. She liked to travel."

"To rather politically charged areas, it would seem. Not your typical vacation hot spots."

"She was interested in the world."

"Our records show she went on twenty trips over eighteen years. Did you accompany her on any of these trips?"

"Very few. I was busy."

"Must have been a lot of legal work to deal with." Kes picked up a stack of papers and flipped through them. "Financials show you were retained for multiple trips at substantial cost."

"Correct, lawyers aren't cheap. Visas, travel affidavits, passports, jurisdictional contracts...I took care of basic requirements to enter and exit other countries."

"Thank you." Kes made herself small and wrote down notes. His shoulders softened. He wasn't perceiving her as a threat; now she could start the interview.

"What was your wife's relationship with Bertrand Silver? It's my understanding that his marriage was flexible?"

"What the hell is this, Francis?" He looked to the captain as if this was a joke.

Kes bit in harder. "Was Peggy having an affair? Is that what brought your marriage to an end?"

"I'm not going to discuss my personal life with you, nor indulge your shameful line of questioning."

"Detective," the captain cautioned her.

Yes to an affair, thought Kes. *No to it being the reason the marriage ended.* She sifted through her papers and slid one across to the Senator.

"There are multiple deposits into Peggy's accounts in the years prior to your divorce, all coming from Slipaway Travel through the personal accounts of Bertrand Silver. Your ex-wife had substantial savings. Not many clients get paid to travel."

"I don't know anything about that." Kes watched his eyes and the thinness of his mouth. *Lie.*

"Payments on her behalf were still being made by Bertand Silver to Willow Glen Care Home, up until his death. He was paying for her care." She looked to the senator and waited.

"Is there a question, Detective?" *He knew.*

"I visited your ex-wife. I understand it was a bitter divorce."

"What are you digging at?"

Kes poked from another direction. "Your net worth, even six years ago, must have been substantial; she should have had grounds for a much larger settlement. But she didn't fight it. Don't you think that's odd?"

"Peggy is out of her mind." The senator leaned in, warning her to back off. "She doesn't meet the criteria of competency."

"That's the lawyer talking." Kes smiled back.

"You're going to stand for this insubordination, John?"

The captain was calm. "Sorry, I was distracted, Senator. I missed that last comment."

"Tell me about Molly." Kes placed the photo of the senator's daughter between them. "Peggy seemed to imply you two were close."

"She doesn't even remember who Molly is. I've had enough of this." But the Senator didn't leave, he wanted an apology. His ego would keep him there until he got one.

"Why were you looking for Molly, Senator? Why didn't she want to be found?"

"Are you a parent, Detective?"

"I am."

"Then you should know parents and children sometimes butt heads. I wanted her home. Quietly and safely."

Kes nodded. "Of course, I understand that." A father worried for the well-being of his child using his influence to get her home. But she didn't believe him. "What was Slipaway Travel transporting from Eastern Europe?" She was nipping at his heels. Driving him to the pen.

"Tourists."

"Why was Molly with Bertrand Silver the last day he was seen alive?"

"What?" Kes saw the senator's flash of confusion.

"Oh, you didn't know that. Molly was with Bertrand Silver the day he was murdered. In his beautiful speedboat. You know the boat, the *No Nonsense*. That's where she was the day you sent me to look for her. Why would she be with Bertrand? Did she know he and her mother had been together?"

"I didn't say they were."

"You didn't have to. All those trips together..." Kes leaned in. "Billie stopped going on those trips and then your wife accompanied him." The senator's jaw tightened; she was under his skin. "Did you have a personal arrangement with Billie Silver? That's what Billie called these affairs, 'arrangements.'" She watched his eyes. *Yes.* "Did Molly know? Or was it Molly who was in a relationship with Bertrand? Another type of 'arrangement.'"

"What the FUCK is going on here, John?" shouted the senator. He grabbed his briefcase and stood. "This conversation is over."

"Two of your former associates are dead, Senator Kinder," Kes said. "Should you be worried? I'm worried for you." He was worried. She stood taller than him. "This is your opportunity to talk. What was your job for the Silvers? Who wanted them dead? Who else are they prepared to kill?"

He was sweating. "You're straddling defamation and slander, Detective. The next time you insist on talking, my lawyers will be with me." He turned on Francis. "How deep is your union's legal pot, John?"

"That's Captain Francis." He didn't get up.

The senator smiled coldly. "Did you know I attend a longstanding poker night? Me, a couple lawyers, a few members of the Advisory Board. Great stress release."

His eyes narrowed like he was taking aim. "You might want to start looking for a new job, Captain." He didn't deign to acknowledge Kes and walked out.

"Jeezus." The captain stared at the table like he was calculating the lawsuit expenses. "That was an utter shit show."

"But now we know." Kes calmly gathered up her paperwork.

"Know what?"

"He doesn't know who's after him. But he knows someone is."

XXIX.

Kes had a couple of hours before she had to pick up Olivia from school. She stopped at her favourite gas station. Family-run, the only one left in the city. Harold, the old man who owned it, or one of his sons would come to the car to chat, wash the windshield, pump gas, and rush back with change. She loved the personal touch. Filling up there always made her feel better, even if there was a long lineup to get to the pumps. She didn't mind the wait; it gave her time to think. She still had nothing on the senator and was nowhere closer to the killer or a motive.

She headed to the Slipaway city office down on the waterfront. As expected, it was locked and abandoned. Billie had made a clean sweep. Likely she had emptied every account to start over again and hid all her assets in some foreign bank.

Kes parked in the empty lot and left the engine running. She had been firing in the dark when she was peppering the senator with questions, hoping for him to reveal a crack in the case, something she had overlooked, but she hadn't gleaned much. She still didn't know why Molly was with Bertrand the day he was killed. If Bertrand and Peggy had been having an affair, could Molly be their child? Did the senator know? Did Molly? What kind of threat would that be to his career and carefully crafted life if it got out that Molly wasn't his? Enough for him to kill? No. He didn't strike her as the jealous type. An affair would reflect nothing on him, he would play the victim. But powerful men don't like to lose. Kes dismissed his involvement. He didn't know Molly had been with Bertrand.

She watched two pigeons scavenging a bag of discarded takeout in the parking lot. There was so much they didn't know about Molly. Chester had said she was born in Central Hospital, but he couldn't access her birth certificate. Maybe it was time for some old-school police work.

Central was an old hospital stuck in an era of sickly greens, yellows, and cheap sixties office furniture. Kes made her way down the windowless hall to the Medical Records Department. She hugged the wall to let a man pass by pushing a floor polisher. She could smell the mustiness of paper before she entered the room. There was nobody at the Records desk. She dinged the bell on the counter and an older man, who looked close to retirement, came out of the back stacks. He was tall and lanky, and under his medical scrubs she could see the collar of his white shirt, and the turquoise clasp of a bolo tie.

She introduced herself and showed her badge. "I'm hoping to take a look at the birth records for a Molly Kinder, born in this hospital." She handed him a slip of paper with Molly's birth date. "A case concerning a missing girl." A small lie.

He looked at the date. "Born twenty-two years ago. That's getting close to the edge. We only keep them ten years after the age of eighteen. Most everything's online now."

"I'd like to see the original records. That would have the birth parents' names, correct?"

"Yes." He waited for her to say more. "You want this now? I was about to go on my break."

"It's urgent." She wasn't going anywhere.

"You'll need to sign in." He pushed a ledger towards her. The page was blank. She flipped back. The last person to sign in was two years earlier.

The attendant put a handwritten note on the door, *Back in 5 minutes*, and locked it. Kes followed him to the service elevator. He swiped his security card. They didn't speak on the short ride to the basement.

The elevator opened onto darkness. The attendant waved his hand and the first set of overhead lights flickered on, revealing a room crammed with shelves stacked floor to ceiling with boxes.

"Motion sensor," he said as though it was a new technology.

Banks of overhead fluorescents crackled and hummed as they walked down the crammed stacks arranged by date. "These are all births?" she asked.

"And deaths and medical files. The records are supposed to be done digitally now, but the doctors and nurses still use paper for the originals. Can't give it up completely. It's faster, accurate, and more personal. Not everything fits in a box." Kes was surprised he spoke so affectionately about the paperwork, like they were diaries and he was their caretaker.

"My favourite are the baby footprints. Even today, they still ink the birth records. The baby's first mark. You can't do that on a computer." He led her through the maze and rounded the corner. "This is the live births section."

He checked the slip of paper and his fingers ran down the boxes. "Year...month...day." He pulled out a box. Inside, the names were ordered alphabetically. He flipped through the files. "K-K-Ki..." He stopped. "Nobody by that name. You have the year right?"

"According to the birth register. Are they normally filed by the father's name or mother's?"

"Usually father, unless there's no father."

"Can you check for Silver, Bertrand...same date."

He looked. No record.

"Maybe the date is off. Could you check Kinder again for the year prior and after?"

He checked the boxes on the next shelf. Nothing.

Kes looked to the endless rows of boxes. "Files must get lost? Or misfiled?"

"I don't misfile paperwork," he said.

"Maybe others aren't as meticulous?" She admired the pride the attendant took in his work, but errors happened. "Or could they have been removed?"

"Paperwork isn't taken off-site. No one comes in here without signing in and being personally escorted. It's more likely your information is incorrect or we never had the file." He put the lid back on the box.

She was back at ground zero. Chester wouldn't have made a mistake with the date. The file was removed, or the date was intentionally falsified to protect someone, or... "If she wasn't born here..."

"You can initiate a search for her birth certificate, but that's through the government. It's all digital now and you'll need the correct name, date, and place of birth for that."

Kes looked to the cardboard boxes reaching floor to ceiling. Somewhere in there was Olivia's tiny footprint. The overhead lights shut off before the elevator door closed.

There was a ticket on the Jag when Kes got back. She tossed it in the glovebox with the others and retrieved the car seat from her trunk. She locked it in place. It was getting to be a tight squeeze in the back seat, even with the passenger seat pulled all the way up. Olivia was growing fast. She patted the Jag's dash reassuringly. "Don't worry," she said, "I'm not trading you in."

XXX.

Olivia came running out of the school, waving back to her friends, her eyes bright with energy. She charged towards Kes.

"You're here!" She hugged her mother's waist.

Kes took in her daughter's floppy hat with a dragonfly pin, striped leggings, woolly sweater, and mismatched socks. "You look lovely, Liv."

"I picked my socks. And I'm wearing your dragonfly!" She nudged aside Kes's jacket hem and touched the badge on her hip. "We're both lovely today!"

"I have a plan for us, before I take you to your dad's."

"What's the plan?" she asked, taking her mother's hand.

"A friend of mine is having a baby. I thought we could go to Diggles and you could choose a gift for the baby and a new book for us to read together."

"That's a good plan." Olivia skipped alongside her. "Is the baby a boy or a girl yet?"

"I don't know." Kes picked her up to tuck her into the car seat.

"I'll choose one that would be nice for anyone."

"That's a good idea. Watch your head, kiddo."

As Kes, fastened the seat belt and straps, Olivia prattled on about her day, her drawings, her favourite teachers, her best friends, and then she shared: "My gym teacher gave me a detention yesterday. He's a dickhead—"

"Olivia!"

She held her ground. "Dad says it."

"That doesn't make it right. What did he do?"

"He was making Donnie run, and Donnie wasn't feeling good, but coach said keep going, and Donnie threw up all over the floor and on Becky. And I told the teacher he was a dickhead for not believing him."

Kes couldn't fault her. "He does sound like a bit of dickhead."

"It was mean of him," Olivia said. "I don't like mean."

She wasn't so unlike her mother after all.

Olivia selected a light brown fox that had a prodigious tail, at least that's what the lady at the checkout called it. For herself, she chose an illustrated book of stories about the sea. She sat in her car seat on the way back and looked at the drawings of an octopus that had taken up residence in a big empty shell.

"Mama, what did the lady at the store call the fox's tail?"

"Prodigious," Kes said, smiling at her daughter in the rear-view.

"What's that?"

"It means large, or impressive in some way."

"Why didn't she say large then? Or huuuuge?"

"People use different words to say almost the same thing, I think she meant it as a compliment. It is a beautiful fox. I think Grace and Chester's baby will love it."

"Prodigious," Olivia repeated and continued whispering the word to herself.

They stopped at a park and ate ice cream while Kes read the book to Olivia. They were both surprised to learn there was a Japanese crab that could grow to be twelve feet wide.

"Come on, Mama. This big?" Olivia held her hands as far apart as they'd go.

"Bigger."

Olivia jumped off the bench and hopped back a few feet. "This big?"

"Keep going."

Olivia took a big step back and Kes waved her farther. Six more steps and Kes said, "Stop. That big."

Olivia eyed the distance between her them. "Wow! That's prodigious."

Kes cracked a beer and settled on the couch. She had on her long woollen socks, not because she was cold, but because of the comfort they gave her. She checked the time. Bjorn was likely in Copenhagen by now. She typed a message: *Hope you've arrived safely*. What could she say? She deleted the text. She had no right to intrude. She looked to her beer and pushed it away. She retyped the message and sent it anyway. He would respond or not.

She looked to the case files strewn on the coffee table and stared at the jigsaw of pieces: photos of suspects, the two victims, the *No Nonsense*, maps of Spectacle, of the world, of Europe, passenger manifests, financials... She slid the photos of Billie, the senator, Bertrand, and Peggy together and set Molly in the middle. She opened the map that she had marked of all the ports Slipaway visited in the past twenty years. She wished she had access to the earlier paperwork. She didn't know much about any of the places.

She picked up her computer and ran a search on their first trip. Bulgaria. She added in the date and scrolled through the archival news headlines: MASS UPRISING, COMMUNIST REGIME FALLS, WINTER OF CHANGE, STUDENT OCCUPATION, EXPULSIONS... She went down the rabbit hole, clicking on articles that took her deeper into worlds she couldn't imagine: ECONOMIC COLLAPSE led to abandoned children to orphanages to stolen children to sold children. Horror stories. She pulled up specific articles involving doctors, nurses, priests, and caretakers, which led to black markets preying on young impoverished mothers...Romania, Bulgaria, Czechoslovakia, Ukraine... There were cases as recently as two years ago. Her phone chimed and she picked it up, grateful for the reprieve.

"Hello."

The phone was silent. She looked at the ID: *Unknown Caller.*

"Who is this?" she said. The line went dead. She hung up and glanced to her door to check that it was locked. She turned off the side lamp and went to the window. All was quiet. It was just a wrong number. She was overreacting.

The sorrowful stories of war and desperation were making her raw. She had investigated too many cases that involved children. Endless pain. It sickened her. Despite all she had seen, all she could shut away, these were the cases that ate her from the inside.

She looked to the cupboard. Three pills to quell the tide of memories threatening to drown her. She climbed onto the stool and grabbed the jar, emptied the nuts and screws, and retrieved the baggy. Her safety net, just in case. Three pills that could dull the pain of seeing.

Three pills. She emptied them into the sink and ran the water hard. "You will not look away." She said the words out loud. "You do not look away."

She gathered her strength and returned to her computer, but the screen was frozen and she was offline. She pressed escape; her keyboard was locked. The phone chimed again.

"I'm not playing this game," she growled.

"Kes, it's Chester! Shut down all your electronics—I've been hacked! They got in through the back door...I don't know how. It's impossible." She could hear him madly typing. "They're inside the case files. I'm shutting them down as fast as I can, but they keep ripping open new entries. I'm trying to trap them. Come on," he said to his computer. "Follow me this way."

Kes knew he wasn't talking to her. She looked to her computer. The internet restored and an article opened on its own, and then another and another...images of war and grieving families, destruction and poverty. She grabbed the map and a pen and frantically circled each country mentioned. She couldn't keep up.

"I think they have control of my computer, Chester!"

"I'm sending a link—click it, I'm taking over remotely... Click it now."

Layers of documents opened, faster than she could read... Ledgers, records? Languages she couldn't translate. Followed by what looked like legal documents. Contracts? Foreign names. Foreign places. Multiple documents blurred past.

Chester was talking to himself: "This way...keep coming...that's it..."

Pages flipped by. Zoomed in. One signature repeated over and over. One name.

Garreth Kinder.

Chester shouted, "Got him!"

Kes's computer flashed and went dark. They wouldn't be able to keep this from the captain. She looked to the photos on the table and edged Garreth Kinder's closer.

XXXI.

Kes and Chester stood at attention before Chief Francis. A heavy morning fog obscured the city and a soft rain was spattering the window. Chester stared at the floor, having insisted that he, too, be there to face the consequences and had made the drive into the city. Kes spoke for both of them.

"Someone made contact last night. Hacked into my computer. Chester..." She corrected herself, "Detective Campbell was alerted to a breach, contacted me, and immediately implemented counter measures to lock it down. I have also been getting calls from an unknown caller, always silent, that may or may not be connected."

Captain Francis stared at his feet through the glass desk. He didn't interrupt.

Kes continued, "They flooded my computer with documents, ledgers, certificates in other languages. Maybe Slavic. All of which were wiped from my device. They accessed the Silver case files, including information on Slipaway Travel. Detective Campbell was able to contain the breach. No data was taken."

Captain Francis raised his hand to stop her, he had heard enough. He glanced out the rain-flecked window. The room remained silent. He looked back to Kes and Chester.

"Can we trace who broke into your computers?"

"No, sir." Chester cleared his throat. "They're good. Really good. They're..."

"...a ghost," the captain finished his sentence.

Chastised, Chester looked back to the floor.

"You opened the door for this to happen, Detective. You assured me you wouldn't leave a trace, that this would not come back to bite my ass. And you..." He checked his notes. "Chester."

"Yes, sir."

"It wasn't his fault," Kes said. "All blame lies with me."

"Yes, it does. I could have your badge. Both of your badges."

"Someone was trying to communicate with us, sir. Just before they were shut down, they were sharing a flurry of documents. Each one signed by one lawyer. Garreth Kinder."

Captain Francis rubbed his forehead like he was fighting a headache.

"I believe whoever reached out knows Garreth Kinder was involved in the same illegal activity as the Silvers."

"Involved how? You saw a name on documents that you couldn't read. Documents you no longer have. From an informant who could be anywhere in the world! Accusations, suppositions, hunches...not one piece of evidence."

Kes looked at him with a cool control. "Why are you protecting him?"

"I'm protecting this *department*! I'm protecting the order of the law!" Kes could see the deep hurt of a man falsely accused. "You want to charge him, you bring me evidence. Admissible evidence! You do the hard work of a detective. Or have you forgotten what that is? Your job is finding out who killed Bertrand and Billie Silver. That's it. Can you stay within that boundary? Can you do your job?"

Kes felt the humiliation of Chester witnessing her reprimand. "Yes."

"I didn't hear you, Detective."

"Yes, sir."

"And you, Detective Campbell..." He stared hard at Chester. "Your services won't be required on this case any longer. I'll need to consider whether there'll be other ramifications. Go home."

"Yes, sir."

Kes looked to Chester and hoped he could see her gratitude, her promise to have his back no matter what happened. It would be okay.

Her phone rang. "Sorry."

It kept ringing. Shrill and insistent.

"Take it," the captain said. "We're done."

Chester glanced her way. She showed him the screen: *Unknown Caller*.

"Morris."

"Hello, this is Matt from the Willow Glen." She shook her head. Not the hacker.

Kes listened. "Is she all right?"

"I'm on my way." She hung up and looked to her captain. "Someone just paid a visit to Peggy Kinder."

Captain Francis sighed. "Well then, why are you still here?"

Chester got in his car and shut the door. The rain had slowed to a drizzle.

"I'm sorry I got you into this, Chester."

He smiled softly. "Wouldn't change a thing."

She reached in her wallet. "Take this for gas. I'll make sure you get paid soon."

"No, I'm good." He put the keys in the ignition and started up the car. "Let me know how it goes."

"Oh, wait." She stopped him. "Olivia and I picked up a present for the baby." She popped her trunk and retrieved the fox. "I was going to wrap it and send it later, but..." She handed it to Chester. "Something small."

"Our first stuffie." He was touched by the offering. He turned it over. "My, what a tail."

Kes smiled. "Yes, it is."

"Thank Olivia for us."

"Will do."

He grinned. "I'm having a baby, Kes."

"Yes, you are. I'll see you around, Chester." It was a promise. She headed to her car.

As Chester pulled away, he waved back with the fox. "Get the bastards, Kes."

XXXII.

On the radio, K. D. Lang was singing a Roy Orbison song. Kes couldn't handle it and switched it off. It was too melancholy, too beautiful. She was pushing the speed limit. The rain had tapered off, but the highways were still slick. She had been on the road for almost an hour and soon would be at Willow Glen.

The entire drive she had been reviewing the fragments she had, trying to piece together the ghost. Who was the informant? Tech-savvy. Intelligent. Hundreds of documents. Obsessive. Driven. All pointing to Kinder. Sent to her. A trail to what?

Forensics hadn't found any prints or DNA at Billie's crime scene. Nothing on the horse trailer door, the box, or the can. No tire tracks or footprints. The bees were purchased, shipped, and delivered somewhere. But she was certain that path would lead nowhere. The killer was careful. Controlled what they wanted to be found. Stalked the victims. Watched them. Waited for the right opportunity. Wasn't in a rush.

It all began with Molly and yet Kes seemed to be wandering farther and farther away from her. She needed to stop chasing the past. She had two murders. She had Molly, the senator, and Peggy. The one true thing she knew was the killer wasn't a ghost. The killer was here.

Matt met Kes at the front door to buzz her in. The entrance hadn't been locked the last time she was there. As she entered, other attendants and nurses appeared in doorways. They were tight with worry. One looked like she had been crying. From down the hall, Kes could hear a high-pitched keening.

"I called as soon as I found her. Well, after the paramedics...we didn't know what happened. But then I called you."

"Who's been in the room?"

"Um, two paramedics, myself, Gennie and Gertie, the nursing assistants...um, that's it."

Enough to have completely muddied the crime scene, Kes thought.

Matt took a deep breath and knocked on the door, slightly ajar. "Hi, Peg. Someone here to see you." He made his voice light and cheerful and pushed it open.

Peggy was sitting in her chair in the corner. She had a bundle in her arms wrapped in a sheet. She was rocking and moaning. A deep agony of grief.

The bed was freshly made and the floor shined as though recently mopped. Peggy's hair was wet and she had on a long flannel gown and slippers. The room smelled of soap and lilac. As Kes approached, she could see that the bundle in Peggy's arms was a doll.

Kes crouched down to her eye level. Careful not to startle her. "Hi, Peggy."

Peggy looked up at her, her face wet with tears. "I had a baby," she said.

Kes looked to the plastic doll with it wide, unblinking eyes. Naked and rigid.

"She's sleeping," Peggy said. "She's just sleeping. This one's not dead. Not like the others." She stroked the doll's cheek. "Wake up, baby. Wake up." And she started to cry and pulled the doll closer.

Kes could feel the depth of the woman's unbearable pain and loss. Wherever Peggy was in her mind, it was true.

"You can't take her," Peggy wailed.

"I won't." Kes stepped back from Peggy's brokenness. She looked around the room, trying to empty herself of the overwhelming sorrow and deafen the heartbreaking cries. Nothing was out of place.

She walked to the ground-floor window and looked down to the wet grass and matted leaves. "Was this open?"

"Just a crack for a little fresh air." Matt sounded as though he was defending himself. "The rooms get so stuffy."

When Kes turned back, Peggy's eyes were closed and she was humming and gently rocking the doll pressed to her chest. Her hand cupped the plastic feet. Kes didn't say goodbye. Matt closed the door behind them.

"That's not how you found her." Kes fought the rise of irritation.

"Once we realized what it was, we gave her a shower. We couldn't leave her like that."

"You didn't think to preserve the crime scene?" *Of course they didn't.*

"We couldn't leave her in that state." He was flustered.

"Tell me exactly what you found when you first went in."

Kes could see he was still in shock. Eyes dilated. Shallow breath. "Peg was on the bed. She was sitting up. Her nightgown had been hiked up to her waist. The doll was between her legs. There was blood…we thought it was blood and called the paramedics, but it was fake, poured over her upper thighs and between…" He froze. His eyes fixed on the memory.

"You're doing good," Kes guided him. "Then what? Just look at me."

He took a breath and focused on her. "The paramedics said there were no signs of injury, just that doll and…"

"Did she say who gave it to her? Male or female?"

"No, she just kept saying it was hers and wouldn't let us take it from her."

"Nobody noticed anyone coming or going? Vehicles they didn't recognize? Unusual calls? Anything out of the ordinary?"

"No. It was like every other day." He paused. "Well, except for our computers. They were down for most of the morning and we were trying to get that sorted out, but they came back on and then we found Peg." He looked to Kes. His face was taut with worry, and maybe fear. "Do you think they'll come back?"

Kes didn't know. The killer had spared Peggy Kinder's life, but there had been no mercy. He'd wanted her to suffer.

"I don't think so," she said, and she could tell he wanted to believe her.

Kes walked the perimeter of the building and stopped at Peggy's window. She had a clear view of Peggy with the doll cradled to her chest. It would have been effortless to open the window and slip in.

The back of the building was ringed by woods, obscuring any approach from this direction. She knew there would be no fingerprints on the windowsill. They would have worn gloves. Planned. Brazen. Orchestrated. The computer crash distracting the staff. Kes's unknown caller wasn't an informant. It was the killer reaching out to her.

She crouched down and ran her fingers through the cool leaves, parting the grass, looking for tracks, but the ground revealed no clues. She stayed crouched, her body tensed, and scanned the woods for any sign of movement. She stood and moved quietly in widening circles, searching the area in a grid pattern. A feather. Deer scat. A mouse trail. No sign of human disturbance.

The woods were quiet with the heaviness that comes after a rain. She breathed in the sweet decay of autumn. *Where are you now?*

Her phone pinged. *Safe and sound*, Bjorn had answered. Maybe, maybe there was a way back.

XXXIII.

It was almost dark when Kes made it home. She was stiff and tired from the long drive up and back from Willow Glen. In just a few days of not keeping up with her exercise and practice, her body felt looser and weaker. She touched her belly like she had done when she was carrying Olivia and was flooded by the image of Peggy clutching the doll. She donned her running clothes and grabbed her backpack. The night was cooler with the edge of a north wind. She headed for Master Jin's. He would be displeased that she had missed these past days. She ran harder to make amends.

Puddles soaked her runners. Street lights came on overhead as she wended through the park. Her fingertips were cold and she could see small puffs of her breath. Without altering her stride, she began the ascent up the long hill. By the time she crested, her lungs were screaming and her calves twitched. She paced until her breath and the cramps in her belly calmed, and her body stopped trembling. She knocked on Master Jin's door. He opened it.

"Oss," she greeted him. She had always loved that word, a combination of *oshi*, to push, and *shinobu*, to endure. "I'm sorry." She waited for his understanding. "I'm ready now." It was time for her to earn the next level.

Master Jin looked her over, then settled on her eyes. Kes tried to still herself and reel in the intensity and distraction of her mind.

"You're still travelling," he said and shut the door.

The shower was hot. Too hot, but Kes didn't turn it down. The room was steamy when she stepped out. She towelled off brusquely. She was angry with Master Jin. He had no right to judge her. He knew nothing about her. She had worked hard and proven over and over how tough she was. And dedicated. And now it was in his hands alone to decide when she could move forward. He was a man, not a deity. *Master,* she had to call him, like she was subservient to him. Her brain corrected her, not *Master. Sensei. Born before. The one who came before.*

Just as quickly as it had come, her anger dissipated. She was the one who had left only to return with her ego, wanting the practice to serve her. She had brought her pain to him. How many times had she stumbled this past week? She was angry that he could look in her eyes and know her truth. The same ability she prided herself on in her own work. It wasn't magic. It was just looking deeply enough beyond what was hidden to see all the lies and hubris.

He was right. She wasn't ready. She wondered how many runs up the hill she would have to make before he opened the door again. *Whatever it takes,* she told herself.

Before heading to bed, she checked her emails on her phone. An attachment from Bjorn. A series of photographs, but no message. She downloaded the images:

a view of Copenhagen through a medieval window, and another at the next level higher, and another, culminating on a wrought iron balcony overlooking red-tiled roofs and spires in the distance. She looked at the series for a long time, trying to imagine what he was feeling.

He was telling her where he was and that he was thinking of her. Showing her part of his world. She looked around her room. How meagre it seemed in comparison. What beauty could she show him? She snapped an image and sent it before she could change her mind. No message. Just an image of a framed photograph on her wall of Olivia laughing.

She quickly scrolled through the rest of her unopened emails, trashed the spam and advertising, before coming to one from Trattoria: *Sorry for the delay. Had to wait for my son to download it. T.*

She switched from her phone to her computer, hesitating only for a moment before trusting that Chester had made it safe. She clicked on the security camera footage. The video started when the restaurant opened. She let it play.

Kes carried the computer to bed, set it up on her side table, and sleepily watched the footage scroll by. The perspective was from the entrance looking back into the restaurant. She could see the table where she and Bjorn had dined. She watched patrons enter and eat, leave, repeat. Her eyes got heavier and she thought she would pick it up again in the morning. But then she saw Bjorn enter and take a seat. Shortly thereafter, she walked in.

It was startling to look at herself. She was wearing a dress. Thomas greeted her, she spied Bjorn and joined him. Others entered and left. Waiters attended guests. Kes had to force herself to watch what else was happening in the room, but her eyes always returned to them, Bjorn and her. Drinks, two. Whisky sours. Wine. Pasta alle vongole for her. Gnocchi for him. How she leaned in. How she laughed. How he talked with his hands. He was sitting with his back to the camera. Him ordering two ports. Her checking her phone. Chester. Her standing up, leaving money on the table. Her leaning over for a kiss. A long kiss. And her leaving, not looking back. Him alone at the table, watching her go. The waiter arriving with two ports on his tray. Setting both on the table and walking away.

Kes was on the verge of tears. She looked to her empty seat and there in the background, facing the door, was Molly. That's how the girl knew they had been there and that she and Bjorn were together. Molly didn't want to take down Bjorn, Molly had used him to hurt her.

Kes sat up, pulled the computer onto her lap, and switched to full screen. Molly was at a table with a man, his back to the camera. An older man. Dark hair, but greyed. Maybe tall, by how he sat in his chair. He had broad shoulders and a suitcoat of sorts, a bit longer than a business coat. He never turned around. Even when waiters approached, Kes couldn't see his profile.

The man reached for Molly's hand across the table and she took his. Intimate. They were leaning towards each other, deep in conversation, and Molly was nodding. The man took something from his wallet and set it on the table. Maybe a photograph? By the body language, the conversation looked intense, maybe even emotional.

Molly picked up the item. She looked up when Bjorn left the restaurant, then turned her attention back to the man, nodding to him as if in agreement. Kes watched the man pay the bill, cash. He donned a scarf and a hat, like a fedora. Old-fashioned in a way, but elegant. When he stood, he was tall and straight-backed. He lowered his chin as he walked to the exit. The hat shielded his face. Just before they reached the door, he put his arm around Molly. *Lovers?* No, it felt more protective.

Molly hugged into him, her hand on his chest, her head down, and the man looked up to the camera and held its gaze. Held Kes's gaze. Proud. A strong face. Dark eyes. She knew those eyes. The man outside of Slipaway. The baying beagle. What had he said? "The hunter. He must have a scent." And now she could hear his accent. Deep. In his throat. The clipped words. European. Eastern European. Czech? Bulgarian? She wasn't sure.

When she first heard him speak, a moment in passing, she'd assumed German, only because so many Germans lived in the area. She peered at her computer screen. The man's straight back. His stride almost military. "They hunt until they drop. Admirable breed." He'd carried his hat in his hand that day. He was in Little Harbour the day before Billie Silver died. And he was in the city, in the same restaurant as her, the day after Bertrand's body was found. With Molly.

Kes went back to the beginning of the footage. She watched herself and Bjorn sit down and eat and drink. She paused and scrolled forward. Molly's table was masked by her. She watched herself lean forward laughing and saw Molly, just over her shoulder, glaring at her back before ducking behind the cover of the man. Kes started again. Rewatched, frame by frame. Molly looked dishevelled, upset. She wiped her face, like she was brushing away tears. A waiter approached their table, and the man held up his hand to wave him back. The man stood and leaned over the table and kissed Molly's forehead before sitting back down. Kes scrolled ahead to when the man looked up at the camera. She hit pause.

"You wanted to be seen," she said. "Here I am. I've been looking for you."

The man stared back.

XXXIV.

The campus was awake with students heading to morning classes. The sun was warming, there was a nip to the air. Kes waited on the bench under the horse statue outside of Molly's dorm. She didn't have to wait long before Molly came out. Her step didn't falter, she almost looked amused.

"Morning, Detective," she said.

Kes raised her face to the sun. "It's a beautiful day, isn't it? Won't be many more of these."

"Has my father hired you to keep an eye on me?"

"No, I wanted to speak to you. Will you have a seat?"

"No." Molly had that invincible air of youth.

"I didn't think so." Kes settled back on the bench. "We have a suspect in the Bertrand Silver case and I think you may be able to give us a hand."

"I've told you all I know."

"I don't think that's true, Molly. I'm hoping you'll come down to the station voluntarily and we can carry on our conversation."

"I have nothing more to say to you. I'm going to be late for class."

"Yes, I think you will be late. You made a false accusation of sexual impropriety by a professor. But he has an airtight alibi." Kes watched the girl's impassive face. "Why would you do that?"

"I don't know." She shrugged. "I was bored."

"Hmm...defamation, mischief." Kes mulled over the potential charges. "I'm sure I can come up with something...it's certainly a civil issue."

"You can talk to my father's lawyers." Molly turned to leave.

"Someone visited your mother, Molly. Did you know that?" Molly stopped. *She didn't know.* "They left a message. Where were you yesterday?"

"In class."

"Aren't you curious whether your mother's dead or alive?" A small trip-up. "You see, I think it has everything to do with you." Kes stood. "You were the last person seen with Bertrand Silver. You and your family are connected to the victims." She walked closer to Molly, who held her ground. "I think this all has to do with the man you met at Trattoria." She had Molly's attention now. "The night the professor and I were there together."

For the first time, Kes saw worry in Molly's eyes.

"If you don't come voluntarily, I'll arrest you right here on obstruction of justice or accomplice to murder at the very least, and see where that falls. I'm happy to call your father or his lawyers to meet us there. How do you want to play it, Molly?"

Kes kept Molly sitting in the interview room alone for twenty minutes. She and Captain Francis watched from the other side of the one-way mirror. Molly appeared composed. Her hands rested on the table, loosely clasped, but she was rubbing her thumb against her palm in a self-soothing motion.

"She didn't want the Senator notified that she was here," Kes said. "And thus far, she has refused a lawyer."

"You don't really think she killed those people?"

"It didn't take strength to drop the bees in with Billie Silver, and she could have been the lure for Bertrand."

"She's twenty-two." Captain Francis sounded weary. His normally starched shirt was wrinkled at the waist. "What has she gotten herself involved in?"

"Let's find out." Kes tucked her file under her arm, filled two paper cups with water, and took them into the room. She sat across from Molly and slid one of the cups towards her.

"Sorry to keep you waiting." Kes took her time setting up. "I'm going to record this session and confirm you have declined a lawyer at this time." She opened her folder and slid the security photo of the man staring up at the camera across the table. "Who is he?"

Molly glanced at the photo. "Someone I picked up. I didn't get his name."

"You seem comfortable with him. Close. His arm is around you, and you're leaning into him." Kes picked up the photo. "You know, I met him once."

Molly swallowed. *She didn't know that, either.*

"Just briefly." Kes set the photo down. "He had an accent. Where is he from?"

Molly's body language tightened. "No idea. I wasn't interested in his accent."

"So, you hooked up for a one-night stand?"

"I was tired of boys." Molly glared back at her.

"Like Lucas?"

Molly scoffed.

"Have you been with a lot of older men?" Kes tried to figure out her game.

"No." Her answer was hard and true. "And it's none of your business."

Kes tapped the photo. "This one *is* my business. Do you believe in coincidences, Molly?"

"No."

"Me neither. This man was in the vicinity of a crime scene."

Kes laid out another image of Molly and the man at the table. The man's hand on top of hers. "You look upset here. What did he say to you?"

Molly remained silent. Kes laid out another photo of the man guiding her towards the door, his arm around her shoulder. "This is so gentle and the other one is almost comforting," Kes said. "Intimate for having just met."

"Jealous?" Molly tried to bait her.

Kes smiled. "Where were you born, Molly?"

"Here."

"Were you?" She didn't wait for an answer. "Have you ever been to Eastern Europe?"

"No."

"You didn't join your mom on her trips with Slipaway?"

"No."

"I was told you were quite close to your father. Your mother told me that." Molly's lips tightened. "Tell me about your mother."

"She liked money and then her brain broke and that was that."

"You weren't close with her?"

"I think she liked the idea of having a child." Molly spoke with the defiance and hurt of a wounded kid.

"Did you know she was involved with Bertrand Silver? That must have been hard knowing she was cheating on your father. Is that what severed your relationship?"

Molly laughed. "You really are a bit of a prude. Rules are different for the wealthy."

"And you *are* wealthy." Kes fanned the photos across the table. "Who is he, Molly? Two people are dead and you're implicated as an accomplice."

"Arrest me, then," Molly challenged.

Kes tried to see through the girl's bravado. "Why are you taking the fall for this man? Do you think he would do the same for you?"

Outside the interview room, a disturbance was getting louder.

"We'll find him, Molly." Kes leaned in. "Help us, before anyone else gets hurt."

Something flitted across Molly's eyes, a vulnerability or sadness that Kes couldn't quite read. The door slammed open and Senator Kinder burst in. Molly's eyes hardened in an instant.

"This stops now!"

As the senator railed and Captain Francis tried to defuse, Kes watched Molly, whose hands were now on her lap. Her head down, which reminded Kes of a small child. The senator grabbed Molly's arm to usher her out.

She pulled away from his touch. "I don't want him here. I don't want his help," Molly said.

As he was escorted to the door, the senator's tirade continued. Threats of legal repercussions, departmental review.

Molly sat quietly, staring at the photos on the table. Kes watched her calm detachment from the ruckus. For a moment, Molly's features softened.

She looked to Kes. "I did it," she said. "I killed them."

The room went silent.

XXXV.

CAPTAIN FRANCIS HAD REMOVED THE SENATOR FROM THE interview room. The last thing he said to his daughter was, "Don't say another word to them!"

Kes sat across from Molly and took a sip of water. "Aren't you thirsty? I can get you something else, a tea or coffee?"

Molly picked up the glass and took a drink. Her hand trembled slightly.

"How did you do it, Molly? How did you kill Bertrand?"

"I asked him to take me for a ride. He loved to show off that boat."

"He's a big man, strong, healthy. How did you overpower him?"

"I'm stronger than I look. Years of self-defence training. My father insisted. One jab to the solar plexus. He couldn't breathe. Knocked him off balance. Dumped him overboard. Wrecked the boat to make it look like an accident." *She doesn't know the details.*

"And Billie?"

"Kicked to death by her horse. Just had to get it riled up."

"How?"

"What does it matter?" Molly pushed back. "She's dead and I did it."

Kes held eye contact, until Molly looked away. *She wasn't there.* The murder weapon, the bees, hadn't been reported. "Why are you lying, Molly?"

"I'm not." This young woman, who had every privilege, was throwing her life away. Why?

"You've confessed, Molly. You'll spend the rest of your life in prison. Do you understand what that means? Your world will become as small as your cell. Not even the senator will be able to help you."

Molly's eyes deadened. "I don't want anything from him." And then she closed herself off. Hard and impenetrable.

Captain Francis was waiting for Kes outside the interview room.

"She didn't do it," Kes said.

It was late and Kes was weary. Weary of the lies. Weary of the chase. She was on the couch staring blankly at the TV, a crappy show regularly interrupted by commercials. She was edgy and had been trying to settle her mind by counting the number of times she had seen the American flag on the program. Twenty-seven, thus far. She would like to call Bjorn, but she couldn't do that. She would like a pill. Her mind roared its assent. She clenched her hands, digging her nails into her palms. She breathed in and out. Stilling her mind, until the craving passed. *Twenty-eight flags.* She tried to focus on what was right in front of her.

A young woman had confessed to murders she didn't commit. Was she counting on her father to get her off with his influence and money? No, Molly hated her father, that much was clear. What had the senator done to her? *Twenty-nine.* Molly had, at the very least, witnessed the abduction of Bertrand. Maybe she didn't intend for him to die. Maybe she wanted to scare him and hired someone to do it? Maybe whomever sent the boat off with Silver lashed to it expected him to be found. Wrenching the wheel off and going overboard wasn't part of the plan. It was still manslaughter at the very least.

Kes pulled the throw over herself and lay down. The room pulsed blue in the television's light. Molly wasn't present at Billie's death. That was first-degree murder. Intentional and planned. *Thirty.* But Peggy was spared. *Thirty-one.* Molly didn't know the killer was still active.

The man in the security footage wanted to be seen. Wanted to be found. He'd been ahead of them every step of the way. Now he was tired of the hunt. Kes shut her eyes as a banner at the bottom of the screen scrolled breaking news about a power outage in the city centre.

Kes woke to the shrill ring of her phone. Just before 6:00 A.M. Her neck was stiff and she was cold. She had fallen asleep on the couch and the throw was tangled at her feet. She fumbled in the dark for her cell.

"Morris." She listened, now fully awake. "I'll be right there."

The TV was still playing on mute. A frenetic morning-show. *Thirty-two,* she resumed counting, as she pulled on her boots.

The police station was on lockdown measures. For so early in the morning, the energy was charged. Street cops, media handlers, and bureaucrats, looking dishevelled having been roused from sleep, crowded the halls. Lucy, the captain's assistant, hadn't arrived for work yet, but her phone was ringing steadily. The captain's office was lit only by a floor lamp, making the room seem to float in the twilight. He was on his phone and waved Kes in.

His coat was tossed in the corner and she was pretty sure he was wearing the same tie he had on yesterday. His cheeks held the bristle where he had missed a spot.

Someone was shouting at him on the phone. He was responding with a detached calm. "I have no influence on them. Yes, it will be everywhere. There's no way of stopping it." The person was talking over him. "It's already been released publicly. We have no way of taking it down. No, the damage is done. Yes, I'll let you know when I do." He hung up and pulled a video up on his phone and handed it to Kes.

Kes hit play. The footage was shot on a phone. A flashlight aimed at the ground, crossing a courtyard. Dark. The camera swung around, held on one building, and moved in closer. The law courts. The flashlight illuminated the head of the statue of Themis, blindfolded, arm high upholding the scales of justice. Stark and white in the night.

The shot panned down to a man—hooded, gagged, and bound—tied to her stone body. Naked. Older. Every roll and bulge on display. His chest heaving with fear. The camera tilted down to the statue's base, where the man had pissed himself, then back to his head. A gloved hand reached in and pulled off the hood.

Senator Kinder. Blinking into the blinding light. His face grotesque with fear. A handwritten sign around his neck: *Guilty.* The shot ended. Thousands of views already. She handed back the captain's phone.

"There's no surveillance footage in the area," he said. "A power outage knocked out all cameras for blocks and when the lights came back on, a cleaning crew on their way out found him and called it in. Ten minutes later, this footage was sent to me and every news outlet in the city."

"Is he alive?"

"Not a scratch on him."

"Where is he now?"

"He was checked over, refused to go to the hospital. He was taken home with a detail. He insists he never saw his attacker. His story is that he was asleep in bed, heard a sound, his head was bagged, and he was brought to where he was found. The alarm system in the house had been disarmed remotely."

"He didn't try to escape?"

"He said a gun was held to his temple."

"Did his assailant say anything to him?"

"No. He said it was a man. He was sure of that. That's it. I'm getting calls from the police board, politicians, and judges who are waking up to the news fearing they'll be next." The captain was still trying to process what had happened.

"How were his hands bound?"

"Rope behind his back. Constrictor knot."

"Same as Bertrand Silver. I'll need to talk to the senator, sir."

Captain Francis nodded. "This has to end." He looked older with his shoulders slumped and his eyes dark with stress. "What are you thinking?"

"Military. Or military trained. The power outage

wasn't a coincidence. Our suspect has sophisticated computer knowledge. He's from the Eastern Bloc. Maybe he worked for intelligence..."

"A foreign agent?"

"The killings are too personal, and now this. Humiliation and public justice. Kinder did something to him. Their paths have crossed. The suspect has been carrying this vendetta for a lifetime." Kes looked up. "Does Molly know?"

Molly was curled up on her cell cot. Her hand was close to her mouth, like she might have sucked her thumb as a child.

Kes unlocked the door and Molly woke with the startle of someone who had monsters in their dreams. She brushed her hair out of her eyes and sat up. Kes stood across from her. They looked at each other in uneasy silence.

"An hour ago, your father was assaulted and found tied to a statue outside of the law courts with a *Guilty* sign around his neck. He's alive. He wasn't physically harmed. It will be on the news. The assailant made a video. You shouldn't watch it." Molly showed no response. "Is there anything you want to tell me, Molly?"

She shook her head no and looked to the floor. Then she started laughing and laughing, which made her laugh harder. Her laughter changed to tears and the more she cried, the harder it was to tell if she was laughing or crying.

XXXVI.

An hour later, the story was on every news channel in the country, with edited versions of the senator bound to the statue accompanied by stock photos of him in stately dress, looking powerfully out to the audience. Kes was sitting in the interview room away from the hum of the station. She had quieted herself and was imagining the statue, the senator, and the binding knots. His mouth gagged. Eyes blinded by the flashlight.

She stared into his irises to see past the light, to see the man. And then she was inside *him*. The killer. Flashlight in hand, pulling the hood from Kinder's head. So close, she could feel the panicked breath of fear. This man he had hunted across time and sea. This coward pissing on himself. How easy it would be to kill him. How much restraint it took not to.

You want something else from him. Kes flickered in and out of his body. She watched the *No Nonsense* speeding into oblivion; listened to the crash of hooves and screams; stood over Peggy dripping fake blood between her legs. She felt only cold hatred and calculated control. Kes looked up to the camera, arm around Molly, heading out of the restaurant.

See me. I'm not afraid. I have nothing to lose.

Kes sat on the bench at the foot of the horse statue. There was a chill in the air. She watched students crossing the quad, computers and books in hand. Young couples, arms around their waists. Rebels and scholars. Some in a hurry, most strolling, deep in conversation on phones or with each other. They all looked so young. Just starting their lives. Believing they had nothing but success to look forward to, that nothing bad would ever happen to them.

Kes watched a man walking towards her. Salt-and-pepper hair, strong features, upright. A tall man, six-foot-two, lean musculature. His face was weathered. He might be considered a handsome man. He could have been a professor. He sat beside her. The cuffs of his woollen overcoat were threadbare and the lining thin. On his feet were well-worn black leather boots.

"I have your daughter," Kes said.

"She's innocent." His voice was soft, held in the back of his throat. His words were clipped with an Eastern European staccato. He removed his hat and laid it on his crossed knee. They watched life in the university carry on.

"That's her room up there. Third floor," he said. "We've had lunch here on this bench." He had a relaxed demeanor. His eyes were the same colour as Molly's, the same nose and skin tone. "I knew you would understand where to find me, Detective."

He looked up to the blue sky and breathed in the sun. "I'm glad I saw the leaves turn colour." He put his fedora back on and stood. "I'm ready. Shall we go?"

Kes stood and two police cars entered the quad.

Anatol Petrov was seated in the same interview chair as Molly had been. Kes sat across from him as they observed each other.

Anatol had been searched and had nothing on him, except for a pack of cigarillos and his wallet. His index and pointer finger were stained yellow from nicotine. She could smell the musky, acrid smoke on his coat. The cameras and audio equipment were recording.

Anatol waited patiently, unconcerned by the gravity of the situation. Kes matched his calm.

"Why do you believe Molly Kinder is your daughter?"

"She *is* my daughter. Taken by the ones I killed." He said it like he was talking about the weather.

"You claim your daughter was taken..."

"The day she was born. Twenty-two years, ninety-eight days. It has taken me this long to find her."

"How did you know Billie and Bertrand Silver?"

"I didn't." He was relaxed. Leaning back. His hands clasped on his crossed knee. Looking directly at her. Every answer was the truth. He was hiding nothing.

"How did you find them?" She kept her voice as soft and casual as his.

"I've been tracking them a very long time."

"Why do you think they took your daughter?"

"Do you know Bulgaria, Detective? What it was like back then? Not just Bulgaria, but Czechoslovakia, Ukraine, Romania, Yugoslavia. Civil wars, protests, everyone was poor. There were orphans, many, many orphans." He recited the information like he was giving a history lecture. Kes didn't interrupt.

"Hard times that you can't begin to know. Children given up by families who couldn't manage anymore. Orphanages filled with sick children, disabled children, traumatized children. Hungry children." He breathed deeply like he was inhaling a cigarette. "There were people who wanted children. But most wanted babies, not children with 'issues,' and there were not so many babies." He told his story with a weary detachment.

His gaze turned inward. "In those days, everything was for sale. There was always someone to be reached with money. A nurse at the hospital. A doctor."

Kes saw a shift, a small crease of his eyes, something closer to his story. "Billie and Betrand Silver?"

He looked back to her with curtained eyes. "You've seen the same shipping routes and financials as I have, Detective." He anticipated her next question. "I was trained in intelligence gathering before things changed, then I had my own security company. Your IT person is very good. Worthy."

Kes hid her unease at the reference to Chester. Too close. Too personal. "Is that how you found them?"

"No. I thought my girl was taken to Russia. Or Europe. I wasn't looking here. I was on every adoption registry in the Eastern Bloc, biological father looking for his daughter, but the records were a mess. Lost, falsified, names changed, confidentiality—I found nothing. But then technology caught up. Six years ago, I spit in a vial and posted my profile on a site. The only leaf on a tree. Three months ago, a DNA match came back. Molly Kinder." His voice softened. "My daughter."

Kes could see the deep ache and wonder in his eyes. "She sent the first message: *Who are you?* She didn't know her world was a lie. How do you tell your child that?" He rubbed the rim of his hat. "Once I found her, I had them, but you helped, too."

"What do you mean?"

"Years ago, I installed monitoring software in the hospital systems I suspected were in the black market of babies. If anyone tried to delete, access, or alter the files, I'd be alerted. They were always silent, until you started looking into Eastern European hospitals, and then I followed you: Slipaway, company records, lawyers...information you triggered, or should I say your partner." She had helped lead him to his prey. She swallowed back the churn of guilt.

"It wasn't your fault, Detective. I had been hunting them a long while. I was going to find them. You just saved me some effort." For the first time, Kes glimpsed the ruthlessness of the man across from her.

"May I take out my wallet?"

He slowly reached in his pocket. The leather wallet was cracked and burnished. He gingerly removed a small black-and-white photograph. It was folded and creased. He opened it gently and laid it on the table for her to see. "This is my daughter, Ana. This is her mother, Katerina." His finger lovingly traced their faces.

It was a photograph of a young woman propped up in a hospital bed, her hair damp, a newborn in her arms. Moments after giving birth. Her eyes were bright with joy. She looked strikingly like Molly.

"We were told Ana died that night." Anatol spoke even more softly. "Our baby girl was so strong and healthy, my wife refused to believe. We begged to see her, but they wouldn't let us."

Kes focused on Anatol's finger lightly touching the infant's head in the photograph. She couldn't look at his eyes.

"I tried to find answers for my wife. I searched the hospital's records. Deceased, that's all it said. Baby girl, no name. She had a name."

Kes looked up, held the fire in his eyes.

"I saw other names of newborns adopted that week, that month. Hundreds that year. From one hospital. How can that be? That many babies unwanted? Sometimes I thought we were wrong, that Ana *had* died that night. It was easier to believe she was gone than live in the limbo of not knowing."

He swallowed down his sorrow, something long practised. "But her mother never, never doubted. She said she could still feel our daughter out there. Three years after Ana was taken, Katerina was gone, too. She couldn't bear the pain." He picked up the photo. "They'll let me keep this, yes?"

"Yes." Kes watched Anatol tenderly slip the photo back into his wallet and tuck it in his coat pocket. "What would you have done if someone had taken your daughter, Detective? How far would you chase them? When would you stop?"

Kes's heart clenched. Was it a guess? Or did he know about Olivia? She felt the danger of him. Real or implied. She bit back the urge to attack.

"Was Molly with you when you killed Bertrand Silver?"

His quiet demeanour didn't alter. "No. She brought him to me, but she didn't know what I was going to do. That's all she did. I sent her away. She wasn't there. She wasn't there for either of them."

"You could have made Bertrand disappear. Dumped his body in the bay. You could have quietly killed Billie."

"I could have." He said it as though it would have been so easy. "But I wanted them found. I wanted people to know how they made their money. The woman, Billie Silver, I remember from the hospital. She was there when they told us Ana died. I remember her. Looking at us. Our anguish. Her eyes, cold." The same cold look, now in his eyes. "They stole my girl."

"And the senator and Peggy Kinder?"

"They bought her. They knew what they were doing. Kinder's name was on all the adoption and travel documents. Papers that said parents voluntarily relinquished their rights. Papers that said mothers died in childbirth, no known family. Lies. He signed for all of them. Dozens of babies. He made his money preying on children. And here in this country, he's a representative of justice?" His eyes were piercing. "So again I ask you, what would you have done, Detective?"

He wanted her absolution. He wanted her to tell him that he wasn't a monster. A cold-blooded killer. He wanted her to validate his justification. Kes held herself still, hid every tell. Held his gaze. Felt the chill of him in her blood. She hid her fear that she would have done the same. She would have hunted them down. She would have never stopped.

"Why didn't you kill him then?"

Anatol leaned back and nodded, like he had his answer and had released her.

"I want the world to know what he did. I want my story told. Our story. Ana's and mine and Katerina's. I want him to lose everything that matters to him. I want him to wish he were dead. That's the only reason he's still alive."

Anatol uncrossed his legs and sat straighter, ready for his judgement. "What will happen to me now?"

"You'll be charged with two counts of first-degree murder and two counts of assault. Charges that could result in twenty-five years to life on both counts."

"I will stay in this country?"

"You will be incarcerated here."

"That's good. Ana can visit if she wants?"

He was going to be locked up for the rest of his life, yet Kes felt no fear in him. He was at peace. "Yes," she said.

"Good. Now let my daughter go."

The data recorder clicked by the seconds. The camera light blazed red. They had everything they needed to convict him.

"It's not that simple," Kes said. "Molly has confessed to the murders."

"She's protecting me," he dismissed her. "You know she's lying."

"If she doesn't recant, she'll be charged as an accomplice."

"Tell her I've told you everything. Tell her Papa needs her to tell the truth now. The rest of my life, I will be here for her."

XXXVII.

KES SAT BESIDE MOLLY ON THE COT IN HER CELL. THEY STARED at the cinderblock wall. Kes told her what Anatol had said and that she knew Molly hadn't committed the crimes.

Molly stared at her feet. She was quiet, just listening. Her eyes filling with tears. "What will happen to him?"

"He'll be arraigned and tried. He'll face a long prison sentence."

"What if I insist it was me? We can't both be guilty."

"Molly, you'll break his heart if you don't live your life."

They sat in the silence.

"They lied to me my whole life. I knew I didn't belong in that family. The way they looked at me. How empty I felt. I thought maybe I was a mistake." Her voice was small and flat. "My birth certificate says I was born here and they're my parents, but it was issued when I was ten. She said the hospital shut down and he had to apply for a new one. They said they named me after my grandmother. Even my name is a lie."

Molly's feet were turned inward like a child on a too-tall chair. Her toes not touching the floor. "It was just for fun, you know. Some of my friends signed up for one of those ancestry kits to see if they had famous relatives or royal blood. So I did it, too. When I checked the results, the first thing that came up was place of origin. It said Eastern European. It highlighted a map in percentages: Bulgaria, Russia, Ukraine. And when I clicked on the results, there was only one match. *Anatol Petrov. Father.*"

"I confronted my"—she corrected herself—"the man I thought was my father. At first, he denied it. He tried to explain it away, how I was legally adopted and that he and the Silvers had helped other children escape to better lives. He said my birth mother had died and my father couldn't care for me and had legally given me up. He said he had helped so many couples, good people who wanted children and children who needed homes. But that's not what Anatol told me.

When I challenged my...the senator, he said I didn't have any proof. He said all the paperwork was in order. People had regrets sometimes, he could understand that, but he was convinced he hadn't done anything wrong. I wanted to know how much I cost. How much does it cost to buy a child? He said I wasn't cheap." Tears spilled down her cheeks. She looked to Kes. "I don't know who I am."

"You have your lifetime to find out. That's what Anatol wants for you."

Molly wiped away her tears. "I didn't kill anyone."

"I know."

"But I wanted to." She sat up straighter, becoming a young woman before Kes's eyes.

"Can I see my father now?"

Through the interview window, Kes watched Anatol and Molly say goodbye. Under the supervision of two officers, they stood apart. Father and daughter, not allowed to touch. Anatol was speaking softly to Molly, smiling through his tears. She was sobbing, and when it was time for him to be booked, she ran forward and hugged him. He eased her away, before the guards could intervene. Kes knew that small action had taken every ounce of strength in his body.

Anatol Petrov was being transferred to a minimum-security prison to await trial. The captain had gone out on a limb, with Kes's lobbying, to make a special accommodation to keep Anatol closer to Molly. He wasn't a flight risk or a danger to others. He would never leave his daughter behind. As Molly was escorted from the room, she promised to visit him soon.

Anatol called after her, "Обичам те."

Molly looked to him. "How do I say it back?"

"И аз те обичам." He smiled.

Molly did her best impression of the deep, throaty sounds, "И аз те обичам," which made them both laugh. "I love you, too," she said again, to make sure it was understood.

Kes stayed, looking through the one-way mirror, long after Anatol was cuffed and taken away.

A squad car was sent to the senator's house to bring him in for questioning. The officers were notified by his housekeeper that the senator had left on business earlier that morning. She didn't know where. He had taken two suitcases and emptied the vault. He had made one call: to inform the Senate he was resigning due to personal reasons. An APB was issued. But it was too late. He'd boarded an international flight to the Maldives, which had no extradition treaty.

Kes was outraged. There was nothing they could do to bring the senator back to face his crimes. She knew she was talking too loudly and her heart was beating fast. She didn't care who was watching through the glass walls of the captain's office. The senator was guilty of child smuggling. Who knows how many families he'd destroyed. Captain Francis sat at his desk and let her vent.

When she paused, he spoke calmly, repeating the facts of the law. The case would be passed on to Human Trafficking, Interpol was notified, Slipaway documents would be seized, but they were advised that in all likelihood, the adoption paperwork would appear to be in order. They paper trail would be legitimate by law, signed by parents who gave up their children. Even if forged, a case spanning back twenty years with no access to foreign records...the odds of proving guilt were negligible.

Kes heard it all and accepted none of it. "We can track down Slipaway's passenger manifests, trace every trip, find them and interview them." Even as her brain tried to find solutions, she knew the cost and manpower required would never allow it. "There have to be other children. Other families who were ripped apart. I'll find them."

"And what then, Kes? What would that do to those children? Look at Molly."

"It's their right to know the truth," Kes bit back.

"That's not our job." There was resignation in her captain's voice and she knew he was right. "All information will be passed to the appropriate departments and agencies. It's their job now to handle this."

Kes was verging on tears. She, who prided herself on being able to hide what she was feeling, felt a helplessness crawling up her throat. She was expected to give up. "So, he gets away with it? And you're fine with that?"

"Of course I'm not fine with that!" Captain Francis's cheeks had reddened and she could see the tremor in his jaw. "It's depraved. It's the worst of humanity. It's incomprehensible. And Molly was one of the lucky ones. She wasn't sold into trafficking or prostitution. Chrissakes!" He slammed his hands down on the table and his voice boomed in the glass room.

Lucy looked up from her desk. Captain Francis motioned to her that all was fine and extinguished his rage. He straightened his coat. He was a realist. He couldn't take on all of life's pain. "Molly is safe here. She goes to university. She has a trust fund. She still has a chance." He picked up a cloth and wiped the smudges of his handprints from the desktop. "We can't save the world, Kes." Words her father used to say.

"Just our corner of it," she added. A phrase she had disagreed with ever since she first heard it as a child.

Outside, a V of geese was manoeuvring over the harbour, practising for its annual migration. Something so enormous and wonderous, yet people barely noticed it.

"I can't do this anymore." Kes set her badge on the glass table.

"Don't be hasty, Detective," he said. "Go home. Take the time you need, and then we'll talk."

She looked to her captain. "Why do we keep trying, sir? The shit never ends."

"Exactly," he said.

She left her badge on the table and walked out.

Kes drove to the city park and found a spot overlooking the ocean. She hoped to see a cruise ship coming into port. She loved watching the tugs and pilot boats greet the massive vessels and guide them to a berth, but the horizon was empty. The parking lot had been restructured and there were barricades impeding access to the views. Fresh bright yellow lines demarcated the parking spots in a dizzying array of uniformity that contradicted the wild of sea and forest. Kes stared out at the darkening sky. She took out her phone, scrolled through her contacts, and dialled the number.

"Nancy, it's Detective Kes Morris… Good, thanks. Off the record, I have a story you might be interested in. There was a prisoner booked today named Anatol Petrov. You may want to talk to him… Yes, I think he'd be open to it. He wants to tell his story… No, I can't comment… Yeah, I think it's big. It goes deep. Nan, I need you to keep me out of this one… Appreciate it."

Kes hung up and turned on the car heater. She made a mental note to get her winter tires installed.

When she got home, a squad car was outside her door. The officer passed her an envelope from the captain.

Inside was her badge. The message read, *You forgot this.* She carried it in and slipped it in her dresser drawer.

EPILOGUE

K̲e̲s̲ ̲a̲n̲d̲ ̲O̲l̲i̲v̲i̲a̲ ̲w̲e̲r̲e̲ ̲o̲n̲ ̲t̲h̲e̲ ̲f̲e̲r̲r̲y̲ ̲l̲o̲o̲k̲i̲n̲g̲ ̲o̲u̲t̲ ̲a̲t̲ ̲t̲h̲e̲ city. The harbour was busy and Olivia loved watching the ships as much as she did. They had eaten all the sandwiches Kes had made for their morning outing. Olivia stood on the deck, leaning into the wind like she was flying. Kes watched her, amazed at how the simplest things in life were always the best. Olivia came running back and plonked down on her lap.

"Was I good, Mama?"

"So good. Aren't you getting cold?"

"Noooo!" Olivia pulled her toque down over her head. "Can we go again?"

"Liv, we've been across three times. We're out of sandwiches and hot chocolate. Aren't you getting bored?"

"Uh-uh. Everything's different every time." She patted her woollen mitts on Kes's cheeks. "Just me and you stay the same."

Kes snuggled Olivia in tight to her as the ferry approached the dock again. She breathed in salt air, autumn fires, winter chill, and her child's sweet smell. Something animal. Something she could never name, but it was a scent she knew she'd never lose the trail of. Her phone pinged and Kes smiled.

It was the last day of fall, and snow was in the forecast. Kes pushed hard up the hill. The night was cold, but she was warm and running strong. She kept her eye on the crest, no distractions, no thoughts, only the pulse of the road. When she could see the dojang, she focused only on the door, the red wooden door, and sprinted the last fifty metres.

Before she reached it, the door opened.

ACKNOWLEDGEMENTS

C. S. would like to thank...

- The South Shore Public Libraries
- All the wonderful independent booksellers
- The Bay of Fundy for its powerful inspiration
- Whitney Moran for her faith in Kes Morris and her diligence and advice
- Retired Corporal Patrick Moran for his procedural knowledge and sharing that with this author
- And Max and Annie for their eternal spirits
- And you, the readers

C. S. Porter is a writer, photographer, and filmmaker who lives near the sea and has passed on that love, fear, and awe to Detective Kes Morris. Their debut novel, *Beneath Her Skin,* won the Crime Writers of Canada Howard Engel Award.